Chloe Scott

SO-BQO-808

The Accidental Orphan

by
Constance Horne

An imprint of
Beach Holme Publishing
Vancouver, B.C.

This book is published by Beach Holme Publishing, #226—2040 West 12th Ave., Vancouver, BC, V6J 2G2. This is a Sandcastle Book. A teacher's guide is also available from Beach Holme Publishing at 1-888-551-6655.

The publisher acknowledges the generous assistance of The Canada Council and the BC Ministry of Small Business, Tourism and Culture.

THE CANADA COUNCIL | LE CONSEIL DES ARTS
FOR THE ARTS | DU CANADA
SINCE 1957 | DEPUIS 1957

Editor: Joy Gugeler
Cover Illustrations: Barbara Munzar
Production and Design: Teresa Bubela

Canadian Cataloguing in Publication Data:

Horne, Constance
    The accidental orphan

(A sandcastle book)
ISBN 0-88878-385-X

    I. Title. II. Series.

PS8565.06693A73 1998   jC813',54   C98-900286-1
PZ7.H67Ac 1998

Chapter 1

On a warm August day in 1885, Ellen Winter stood on a crowded dock in Liverpool gazing out at the steamship *Lake Superior*. All morning, she had been selling flowers to people boarding the small steam launch that taxied them out to the great ocean liner. Should she wait for her to sail or head home with the day's profits? She glanced down at her basket. Only two nosegays were left. "Not much hope of selling these now," she muttered. The passengers had all gone out to the ship. Those waiting to see them off wouldn't buy flowers for themselves and neither would the people shopping at the stores that filled the street level of the big warehouses across from the dock. "Don't matter though, I've made enough to buy three lamb chops for Uncle Bert's tea!"

"I'm off," said an old toffee seller named Sal whose tray was almost empty. "It's near time to get my tea."

"Uncle Bert will be at the theatre for hours yet," said Ellen. "They're rehearsing a new show today."

"Playing his fiddle, is 'e?"

Ellen nodded and watched as her friend threaded her way through the crowd. It was almost noon and the water taxi had just one more trip to make out to the steamship. Ellen had learned to recognize the uniform of the harbour pilots who guided the big ocean liners down the Mersey River and through St. George's Channel toward the south coast of Ireland. Near the city of Wexford the captain of the liner would resume command of his ship and the pilot would be set ashore to guide another big vessel back up the Mersey to Liverpool. Ellen knew that the pilot always went out on the last trip to the ship. One was standing nearby talking to the crew. Ellen heard him ask, "What are we waiting for then Jim?"

"A pack of orphans from the workhouse, I'm told. Going off to make their fortunes in Canada, or so they say."

The pilot grunted. "Well if they don't hurry, they'll be left behind. The tide'll turn in 'alf an hour and His Nibs, the Captain, will want to catch it!"

"Here they come," chuckled another sailor. "'Appy looking lot, ain't they? Here you," he called to a man who was slowly pushing a hand cart loaded with two large wicker trunks. " 'Urry up! Get that luggage aboard!"

Ellen stepped back as the porter pushed his way to the side of the launch. Behind him marched a thin, sour-faced woman. A string of orphans tramped two by two after her except for one girl who marched alone. Ellen moved farther back into the crowd. She didn't want to be anywhere near those 'workhouse brats.' For the hundredth time she thought how lucky she was to have Uncle Bert. Even though her mother and father had been dead for three years, no one could call her an orphan and put *her* in the workhouse as long as she lived with him.

The orphans had come to a halt beside the launch. There were seven of them, four boys and three girls. They all seemed to be about Ellen's age, eleven. In spite of the warm day the boys wore navy pea jackets, woolen shorts, grey caps and long grey stockings. The girls were dressed in three-quarter length grey woolen cloaks over brown dresses with grey bonnets on their heads.

She wondered if they were glad to be getting away from that old dragon. Well, who wouldn't be! But, maybe they'd be worse off where they were going. It must be awful being an orphan. She winced in sympathy when the dragon lady's harsh voice said, "Attend to me!"

"Yes Mrs. Wickham," chorused the children.

"You will go on this boat over to the liner. Miss Fawcett is already aboard. She will meet you there. She will be in charge of you from now on." The matron paused.

"Yes Mrs. Wickham," said the orphans.

"It is very good of her to take charge of you on your journey."

"Yes Mrs. Wickham."

"You will obey her at all times."

"Yes Mrs. Wickham."

"You are very fortunate to be going to new homes in Canada."

"Yes Mrs. Wickham."

"You are grateful to the Society here which made the arrangements for you to go to Canada."

"Yes Mrs. Wickham."

"You are grateful to the kind people who will give you homes."

"Yes Mrs. Wickham."

"You will remember all these people in your nightly prayers."

"Yes Mrs. Wickham."

"Goodbye children," she said with the same stern expression she had worn throughout.

"Goodbye Mrs. Wickham."

One by one the orphans stepped into the launch. Mrs. Wickham turned away and marched off down the dock. The children relaxed slightly. Two of the boys exchanged sly grins.

Ellen was smiling with them when she was suddenly pushed violently from behind. Off balance, she staggered a few steps. "Run!" a voice hissed in her ear. Something heavy dropped into her basket. She looked up in time to see a boy dressed in rags dart between two men and race away down the dock. "Stop, thief!" someone bellowed behind her. A slim girl dodged in and out among the crowd and sent Ellen flying again. She fell against a dock worker, badly crushing her straw hat and dropping her basket.

When she bent to pick it up, the bellowing voice seemed closer. "Stop, thief! Hold that girl!"

A man grasped Ellen's arm. Another man, quite stout and wearing a blood-spattered butcher's apron, panted as he came up to them. "Ah thankee mate," he puffed. He took a painful hold of Ellen's other arm. "The little varmints! Always stealing me bangers. Three times this week alone! Ah well, I've caught you now, eh?" He shook Ellen violently.

She stared at him in horror. "No, no," she said. "I didn't... I've been selling flowers... I...,"

He twisted her arm cruelly. "Aye," he said, "I've seen you! Standing around with your wee basket ready to hide the goods!"

"No, no," Ellen said. She tried to pull away from him. "I didn't steal anything I tell you!" Tears filled her eyes and she tightened her grip on the handle of the basket.

The butcher reached a huge hand into it and pulled out a length of sausages. "What's this then, eh? What's this, Missy?" he demanded in a loud voice.

Ellen gazed at the pink, greasy links in amazement. Her face felt burning hot and her back cold as ice. She looked up imploringly at the purple face of the angry man. Finding no sympathy there, she cast quick, frightened glances around at the people who had turned to see what the commotion was about. They were only mildly interested. Gangs of young thieves were common in the city. It was not an unusual sight to see a little girl in the grip of an angry merchant.

"It's the workhouse for you this time, and no mistake!" said the butcher. "Ah, see there! The copper's caught the lad! Good! Good!" He hauled Ellen, squirming and struggling, toward a policeman.

At the sight of the boy, Ellen's terror turned to anger. "Why did you put the bangers in my basket?" she demanded.

"Why, you told me to Sis," the boy answered in a surprised tone. "Don't you remember? You told me to toss the goods into your basket quick as I could. In case I got caught, a decoy you said."

"You liar..." began Ellen. Her words were cut off by

another violent shake.

"Ah, there, did you hear that?" the butcher asked the policeman triumphantly.

The officer nodded gravely. "Yes. I expect they've had lots of practice. Bring them over to your shop and I'll write up the details for the magistrate."

While the children were dragged along toward the stores, Ellen hissed at the boy, "Why did you say that?"

"Don't be a dummy," he answered in a quick, fierce whisper. "Do you think I want them to look for me sister? How'd our Ma feed the young 'uns if we're both away to prison?"

"Pipe down you two," said the policeman.

They stopped beside a brazier outside the butcher shop. Chops were grilling over a low fire. The smell reminded Ellen of Uncle Bert's tea. She gulped. Who would cook his meal if she went to jail? The policeman handed the boy over to the butcher and pulled out his notebook and pencil. While the two men talked above their heads, Ellen began to tremble. Oh, if only Uncle Bert were here! She saw the butcher's fat stomach and the boy's face blur through her tears.

"Please, not prison," she sobbed.

"What a dummy you are," the boy muttered. "We ain't going to prison! Look sharp and be ready to run."

The butcher was holding each of them by the arm as they stood with their backs to his shop window. The policeman, balancing on one leg to use his knee to write on, was a few feet from Ellen on her right. To the left, beyond the boy, were the glowing coals of the brazier and a pile of tarred rubbish from the marine supply store next door.

Ellen blinked to clear the tears from her eyes. The boy winked at her. She tensed herself for flight. Suddenly, the boy kicked the butcher's shin and swung his free fist hard into the man's middle. The butcher dropped both children and grabbed his stomach. Ellen lurched ahead and raced toward the waterfront. The boy darted sideways and kicked the grill over onto the rubbish. Instantly, a fire blazed up. The startled policeman and the butcher collided in mid-chase the instant they saw the fire.

Ellen heard shouts behind her as she ran. "Fire! Fire!" Fire was a terrible menace in the dock area where many warehouses were crammed with flammable goods. While no one paid much attention to the capture of thieves, everyone on the dock turned to watch the fire. All this had taken only a few minutes, even though it had seemed to Ellen to be a never-ending nightmare.

Pausing for breath, she found herself beside the launch loaded with orphans. After ordering the children to stay put, the pilot and crew had run to see if they were needed to help put out the fire. Everyone was looking in the direction of the butcher shop. Ellen looked around wildly for a place to hide.

"Psst! Here!" came a voice from the boat. A red-haired girl crooked a finger at her. Ellen hesitated. If she hid on the boat, how would she get off when the crew returned? Her eyes darted from the girl to the fire. It had been contained. The crowd stirred and moved away. The butcher's loud voice bellowed again. "Where's the little devils? 'Ave you seen 'em? I'll fix the beggars!"

Ellen leaped into the boat. Her battered hat and the flower basket flew into the filthy harbour water. She landed against a crate with a crash that stunned Ellen for a moment. Three girls bent over her and the one who had beckoned quickly undid her cloak and threw it over Ellen. Another girl removed her own bonnet and fastened it on Ellen's head. Several hands fumbled together trying to push Ellen's long, brown hair up under the hat. The redhead slapped them all away and did it herself. Then she rummaged around in the trunk for an extra cloak for herself. Each of the orphans had been supplied with two uniforms, but only one hat.

"You'll just have to say your hat blew off, Melly," said the redhead as she fastened her cloak.

Just then the crew returned in a hurry to get out to the liner. The men were furious at the youngsters who had started the fire.

"Might of burnt down the 'ole place. Should be in jail, both of 'em!" said one sailor as he cast off.

All the way out to the liner, the pilot and the sailors discussed the punishment for thieves and arsonists. They paid no attention to the children. Ellen was whispered to by her rescuer, introduced as Hannah Webb. She seemed to be the leader of the group.

"I'll think of something," she said, when Ellen asked her how she was to get back to shore.

Soon the side of the liner loomed up beside them. A sailor fastened one end of the collapsible stairway to the rail of the launch.

"Up you go younguns," yelled the pilot. "Ladies first! Step lively now! No hanging back! We're in a hurry here."

Ellen was trapped. In order to stay on the boat and return to Liverpool she would have to admit who she was. She knew that the sailors would turn her over to the police as soon as they reached the dock. Yet, she couldn't sail to Canada on the steamship. How would she ever get home again?

Hannah poked her forward. "We'll figure out something later," she whispered. "Just go up now."

On the deck of the liner the group was met by a worried-looking young woman, presumably Miss Fawcett. She was pulling at the chain of her pince-nez glasses which was tangled up in her bead necklace. She finally perched the glasses on her nose and greeted the children.

"You're very late," she said.

"Yes Ma'am," answered Hannah. "You see, Jane Potts came out in spots this morning. The wardens decided to leave 'er behind and send the rest of us. I was supposed to tell you."

"What do you mean?" asked Miss Fawcett. Her glasses had fallen off and she held them up to her eyes and peered at the children. "There are *eight* of you."

Ellen spoke up. "I don't belong with them. I have to get off. I don't want to go to Canada."

"Don't be foolish girl," said Miss Fawcett. "You should be grateful to be going to a new life in Canada. Not many orphans get such a chance."

"I'm not an orphan," declared Ellen, hotly. "I'm just here by accident. See? I don't have a workhouse uniform!"

She snatched off the hat and thrust it at Melly, then dropped the cloak to the deck, revealing a dark blue dress and shabby blue buttoned boots.

Miss Fawcett frowned. "What is the meaning of this?"

Ellen and Hannah began to talk at once. The woman waved her hands distractedly. *"One* of you tell me," she said.

Ellen explained at length exactly what had happened on the dock. Just as she finished, a prolonged blast of the whistle sounded from far above them.

"There, we're sailing!" declared Miss Fawcett.

"Oh no! I have to get off!" cried Ellen wildly.

She raced to the railing. The buildings of Liverpool were slowly retreating. The *Lake Superior* was on its way to Canada.

Miss Fawcett had taken the job of escorting the orphans in exchange for free passage to her elder brother's homestead near Morris, Manitoba in the far western part of Canada. According to her employers, she was to have a worry-free voyage, but here was this wretched girl with a *very* big problem! Miss Fawcett thought Ellen was quite likely a thief. All the more reason to get rid of her. She left the children in the lounge and went in search of a ship's officer.

When she returned she had good news. "The pilot," she said, "leaves the ship as soon as we're through the Channel. You may go with him to Wexford and he'll take you back when he guides another ship to Liverpool."

"When?" demanded Ellen.

"I beg your pardon?" said Miss Fawcett in an icy tone.

Ellen's cheeks burned. She took a deep breath to control her impatience. It would do her no good to make the lady angry. Politely, she said, "I mean, Ma'am, when does the pilot leave the ship, if you please?"

"Early tomorrow morning."

"Tomorrow! But I have to go back to Uncle Bert!" burst out Ellen, forgetting her resolve to be polite. "He won't know what's happened to me. He'll be worried."

"You tiresome child," scolded Miss Fawcett. "I'm *trying* to return you to your uncle! And I'm sure it's more than you deserve. Now, listen to what I say!"

She explained that Ellen would be awakened early in the morning and put in the pilot's charge. Ellen remembered his angry talk about thieves when he learned they had started the fire, but she was sure, if she could just get home, Uncle Bert would straighten all that out. She would much rather take a chance on the pilot than sail to Canada!

The afternoon and evening passed very slowly. Ellen went to bed in the cabin with the other girls, but she couldn't sleep. Her mind kept going over the events of the day. She wondered what Uncle Bert had done when she didn't come home. Was he out looking for her this very moment? He must be worried. She longed for the morning. At last she dozed off, only to be awakened by the blare of the ship's foghorn. The sound became part of her dreams. Sometimes it was the butcher shouting, "Stop, thief!" Sometimes it was her uncle calling, "Ellen, where are you?"

At last, she thought it must be morning. She dressed and hurried upstairs. When she stepped out on deck, cold wet mist clung to her face and hands. She could barely make out the railing only a few feet away. Except for the regular groan of the foghorn, it was quiet. Had she been forgotten? Had the pilot gone ashore without her? The dampness made her cough. Suddenly, a sailor loomed up out of the fog.

"What are *you* doing here?" he demanded.

"Has the pilot gone ashore?" asked Ellen.

"What? In this pea soup? He don't even know where Wexford is!" He took Ellen's elbow and led her back to the door. "Now get inside. There's a good lass."

The morning dragged on. All the passengers were talking about the weather. "Worst fog I've ever seen," said one.

"I'm scared!" said Amanda, another orphan.

At last, by mid-afternoon, the ship steamed out of the fog. Several passengers cheered when they saw the sun again. A few minutes later the pilot entered the lounge. Ellen leaped up and ran to him.

"Here I am," she said. "Are we going now?"

He looked down at her blankly. "Eh? What? Oh, you're the little lass who wants to go back." He shook his head. "No, we're going nowhere. That is, we're going to Quebec. We missed Ireland in that fog. Never saw the like. Ah well," he said, shrugging, "I've no objection to a free passage to Canada. Give me a bit of a rest, it will." He turned away, laughing.

White-faced, Ellen stared after him. "I can't go to Canada," she whispered. "I have to go *home!*"

But the *Lake Superior* sailed relentlessly on.

Chapter 2

Miss Fawcett was almost as upset as Ellen. Not knowing what else to do, she decided to treat her as one of the group. Ellen hated this, especially when Miss Fawcett insisted that she wear the uniform. Luckily, there were no extra shoes, so Ellen had to wear her own blue boots. She would often sit with her feet thrust out so that people could see them. Surely this made it clear she was *not* an orphan!

There was nothing Ellen could do about returning to Uncle Bert as long as she was on the liner. "As soon as we land at Quebec," Miss Fawcett promised, "I shall cable the Secretary of the Society in Liverpool and ask him to find your uncle. What's his full name? Herbert Winter? He can say what is to be done with you."

One of the orphan boys, George Matthews, always snorted when Ellen boasted that she was not an orphan because she had an uncle. One morning the children were sitting on the floor of the aft deck, their backs leaning against huge coils of rope that smelled of tar. Ellen had just told them about the time Uncle Bert had taken her to see a circus. Melly and Fred were very impressed.

"I'm going to a circus someday!" declared Fred.

"I hope you will," said Ellen kindly.

George looked sour. "I don't believe you 'ave an uncle," he said.

Ellen was outraged. "I do so!" she declared.

"Well, anyway, you ain't got no mother or father," he said. "You're an *orphan.*"

Ellen jumped up. "I'm *not* an orphan, George Matthews!"

"Well, you're dressed like one."

"No, I'm not! Look at my boots!"

"Pooh! What's boots! I say you're an orphan." He stared up at her daring her to prove that she wasn't.

Ellen sputtered with rage. "How can I be an orphan when I've got Uncle Bert?" She glared at him.

George stood up, stepped over the outstretched legs of Albert and Fred and faced Ellen squarely. They were about the same height so when he put his hands on his hips and thrust his face forward, they were almost touching nose to nose. "An uncle doesn't count as family!" he taunted.

Ellen took a deep breath and held it. Her forehead turned hot as she tried to think of something mean enough to say. She let out her breath with a whoosh and swung her right hand flat against his cheek. George yelled and grabbed her long hair. The other children jumped up and surrounded them. Fred and Albert grinned. They liked watching a scrap. Giggling, Melly moved out of the way. "You'll be punished if Miss Fawcett catches you," warned Amanada, but neither

Ellen nor George heeded her. Hannah stepped in, saying, "Now, don't fight! Somebody will get hurt." Just then George gave a great tug at Ellen's hair which brought her head smack into Hannah's. Hannah retreated in tears. Ellen moved in close to George to ease the pull on her hair. She pounded both fists, with all her strength, on his back and shoulders. "I do SO have an uncle! I do SO!" she gasped. She poked an elbow into his right eye. He let go of her hair and returned the blows. She kicked him hard in the shins.

Lanky Bill, slow to think and slow to move, finally decided to intervene. Fortunately, George had ears that stuck out. Bill grabbed them and pulled back until George could no longer reach Ellen.

Still holding George by the ears, Bill said, "You shouldn't fight a girl."

"Leggo of me, you big lummox! I'd have beat her if you'd let me alone."

Suddenly Hannah hissed, "Hush! Fawcett!"

They all heard the clinking of the beads against the glasses' chain as she came up behind them. Anger made the end of her nose pink.

"What is the meaning of this?" she asked, scandalized. "Fighting! I'm ashamed of you!"

Bill let go of George. The children all moved closer together.

"This is disgraceful behaviour!" she went on. "George Matthews, look at me. A boy who's been given a great opportunity and you behave in this fashion! Aren't you ashamed of yourself?" George scowled at the deck boards. "Aren't you ashamed of yourself?" she repeated shrilly.

"Yes Ma'am," muttered George.

"I should think so!" Turning to Ellen, she said, "As for you, Ellen Winter! Whatever made you do such a thing?"

"He called me an orphan," Ellen said angrily.

"Stop! I don't want to hear another word!" Miss Fawcett took several deep breaths while clutching her necklace. Finally, she exclaimed, "Fighting! Young ladies don't fight!"

"I ain't a young lady," said Ellen.

"You certainly aren't," snapped Miss Fawcett. "Go to your cabins, both of you, while I decide how to punish you."

At first, Ellen was too angry to cry. She lay on her bunk and seethed. George Matthews was hateful! Her scalp hurt where he had nearly pulled out a chunk of her hair by the roots. Her forehead ached where he'd knocked her head against Hannah's. There was a bruise on her upper arm where he'd pounded her. But none of these hurt so much as the fact that he didn't believe in Uncle Bert.

"I hate him!" she muttered. "I hope he goes to the meanest family in Canada!"

Miss Fawcett made them go without food for the rest of that day. The next morning, between prayers and breakfast, she lectured the two of them with stern words and then allowed them to rejoin the other children.

A few days later, land was sighted. "That's Newfoundland," an officer told them. "Tomorrow we'll be in the St. Lawrence River and then it's just a short way to Quebec." The passengers cheered. They were almost there!

In the morning, the orphans lined up along the ship's rail with the other passengers. Quebec City looked beautiful. Stone and brick buildings along the waterfront shimmered mysteriously through the light mist, while high on the cliff the buildings were bathed in a rosy-red glow from the early morning light. Forests and green fields surrounded the city. The new country!

"Canada!" said Hannah softly.

When they disembarked, Miss Fawcett kept her promise about sending a cable to Liverpool, but Ellen was astonished when told that the answer might take several days. In the meantime, she had to go on with the orphans to Toronto.

"I can't go on the train, Ma'am!" she protested. "Uncle Bert will expect me home on the next ship. I'll have to be near the dock."

"Nonsense," said Miss Fawcett crossly. Her pince-nez glasses fell off her nose and swung on their chain. "Don't be tiresome! Where would you stay in this city? The Society has no contact here. You will come with us to Toronto." She pushed Ellen firmly into line. "I've asked the Secretary to cable me at the Home there." She took her place at the head and the children marched behind her toward the railway station.

Ellen's mind was whirling. She must get back to the ship! She could sneak on board and hide. If she could stay hidden until the ship had sailed out to sea, they'd *have* to take her home!

The group crossed the road and approached the doors of the station. Ellen let a porter with a loaded cart push in front of her. Shielded, she stepped sideways and took off at a run back towards the harbour, dodging in and out among the people hurrying along the street.

Behind her, she heard George's hateful voice. "Oh, Miss Fawcett! Ellen Winter's 'opped it!"

"What?" said the young woman sharply. "Ellen! Ellen Winter, come back here!"

Ellen ran faster. People turned to look at her. She heard Miss Fawcett order, "Bill, go fetch her!" She looked around wildly. An alleyway opened on the left. She darted in only to find herself up against a brick wall. She whirled around and took a few steps back toward the entrance. Bill and a policeman appeared before her.

"Where are you going Ellen?" Bill asked.

"I was trying to get back to the ship," she said, glancing uneasily at the policeman.

Puzzled, Bill walked along beside her back to the others. "Why did you want to go to the ship?" he asked.

"I want to go home," she almost shouted. "I was going to stowaway on the boat."

Bill spoke slowly. "If they catches you, they'll put you in prison."

Ellen shuddered. Prison! What if the butcher was waiting on the dock when the ship reached Liverpool? She couldn't be a stowaway; she'd have to go on with the orphans and wait for an answer from her uncle.

The answer came three days later in Toronto when George and Ellen were the only orphans not yet placed with families. Ellen was called to the office of Mrs. Macready, the Matron of the Home where they were staying. Miss Fawcett was standing at the window with a piece of paper in her hand. Even before she spoke, Ellen knew it was the cable from England. She pressed the palms of her hands together to stop their trembling.

Miss Fawcett said, "Listen to this, Ellen. It's from the

Society secretary. 'Be advised that we can find no trace of
Herbert Winter. He left his lodgings several days ago, leaving
no forwarding address. Theatre reports he has not been at
work since August seventh, the day the S.S. *Lake Superior*
sailed. He seems to have vanished. Society approves your
conduct re: the minor, Ellen Winter, and authorizes you to
continue to treat her as an orphan. In the absence of her
uncle, she is indeed an orphan of this parish. Therefore, let
her take the place of Jane Potts. You have our full authority
to place her where you and Mrs. Macready think best.' It's
signed, S.E. Edmonds, Liverpool Society for the Placement
of Deserving Orphans in the British Colonies."

During the reading of the cable, the blood had drained
from Ellen's face and her eyes had opened wider and wider
into a fixed stare. Miss Fawcett looked at her. Ellen shouted,
"No! No! I won't be an orphan!"

"Ellen Winter!" scolded Miss Fawcett. "Behave yourself.
What will Mrs. Macready think of us?"

"I think you have a very undisciplined child here, Miss
Fawcett." She looked thoughtfully at Ellen. "I wonder if
there ever *was* an uncle?"

"Perhaps there was," answered the younger woman, "and
he's taken the opportunity to escape from his obligations."

Ellen choked back a retort.

"Isn't it lucky that there is a place for her to go?" the
Matron said.

Lucky? Hateful woman! Ellen clenched her teeth.

"I know it's sad for you not to hear from your uncle,
Ellen," Mrs. Macready went on, "but once you're established
in a comfortable new place, you'll soon forget all about him

and be happy with your new family. You'll be going to a farm out west, you know. You and George will be the first orphans we've ever sent out there, so you will be ambassadors for the Society. Naturally, we expect you to be good ones."

I don't want to be an ambassador for your old Society, thought Ellen. I want to go home!

Chapter 3

Three days later, in Winnipeg, Miss Fawcett said goodbye to Ellen and George. From here, she was going south to her brother's farm near Morris and the children were going farther west. At the station, the young woman made sure that the two small tin trunks, packed with winter clothes and a Bible, went into the baggage car. Then she pinned name labels to the children's shirts and marched them up to the conductor.

"These two are going to Patterson," she said. "Someone will meet them there. Please see that they get off the train."

"I will Ma'am," answered the man with a smile. "They'll be safe with me."

He touched the peak of his flat cap to the lady, then turned and winked at the children. Ellen was glad to hear the clicking of Miss Fawcett's beads fading in the distance.

After the train left the city, the landscape became more and more open and flat and less and less populated.

Occasionally a farm house could be seen on the horizon or they would go through a tiny town. The vast, empty spaces frightened Ellen who had lived all her life in a crowded city. How could she ever find her way home from here?

"Cor, it's empty!" she exclaimed aloud, after an exceptionally long stretch without a sign of human life. She was talking more to herself than to George, but he answered her as if he too had been depressed by the view.

"Kind of lonely looking, eh?" He paused a moment. "Well, cheer up. Our farms may be near a village."

"Or they might not be," answered Ellen.

"Don't be so gloomy!" said George. "Maybe you'll be part of a big family. You won't be lonely in a big family."

Ellen didn't answer aloud, but she thought, "Yes, I will be, if they don't like me. If they laugh at the way I talk. And don't believe in my uncle in England. If they expect me to help with the farm work even if I don't know how. I'll be an outsider, and I'll be lonely."

"Next stop Patterson! Patterson next!" called the conductor, as he walked through the coach. He winked at the children as he passed. "That's you. Ready?"

Ellen nodded. She wondered who would meet her. Would they like her? Would she like them? When the train stopped, the conductor grasped Ellen's elbow as she took the long step down to the platform. To her surprise, her knees nearly gave way.

"Steady!" he said. "Bit nervous, eh? Well, best of luck! You too, young chap," he added as George followed.

Ellen took a quick look at George and saw that all the color had drained from his face.

On the small platform a number of people stood staring at the train and the two small passengers who had disembarked. Two men came forward. The young one was dressed in overalls and farm boots. He had merry blue eyes and a face browned by the sun. The other was much older, with an unshaven face and dirty overalls. His eyes were hard and cold.

"These the orphans?" the younger man asked the conductor. "I'm Bill Aitken."

"And I'm Alf Black," said the other in a gruff voice.

Don't let it be him, prayed Ellen. Oh, please, don't let it be him.

"Yup! This is them," answered the conductor. He drew Ellen forward. "I believe the girl is yours Mr. Aitken. Name of Ellen Winter, as you can see."

"Hello Ellen," said the young man.

Relief and shyness kept Ellen tongue-tied for a moment. Then she managed to say, "How do you do Mr. Aitken."

"Call me Bill," he said with a laugh.

"And this is George Matthews, Mr. Black."

The farmer nodded to the boy and asked the conductor what luggage he had. When he had pointed out their boxes, the conductor called, "All aboard!" and the train pulled away.

Soon George was driven off in a farm wagon and Ellen felt really and truly alone. Although she hadn't liked him, George was her last link with home. She looked after him wistfully and half-raised her hand to wave farewell. In another few minutes, the town was left behind and she and Bill Aitken and the horse, Prince, were alone in the vast emptiness.

The afternoon was hot, and the seat hard and slippery. Bill apologized for the wagon.

"I came into town yesterday for grain sacks. The station master gave me the telegram saying you'd be coming in on today's train, so I decided to stay over and meet you instead of going back and forth. The buggy'd have been the proper rig for a lady, I guess." He smiled at her.

Ellen gave a tiny smile. "Is it far to your farm?" she asked.

"Far enough. We don't go into town every day. But you're not going to my place, you know."

Ellen felt cold all over. "No?"

"No. You're going to my parents' farm. See, I'm just a bachelor, homesteading on the next quarter to Dad's. I have to live there for three years and then I'll own the land." He grinned down at Ellen, who had jounced along the seat until she was almost under his elbow. "You don't know what I'm talking about, do you?"

Ellen pushed herself back to the far side. She shook her head.

"Never mind. You'll learn all about it one day. My sister Hilda is the school teacher and she loves to explain things."

"Am I going to live with her?"

"Well, she lives at home most of the time—except in the winter. But, it's our parents you'll be living with. Them and May, my little sister. She's thirteen. How old are you?"

"Eleven."

"Mmmm. Don't let her boss you. You'll get enough of that from Miss Hilda and from Mum."

Ellen was silent. The heat and the bouncy ride and worry about the future were making her feel faint. Bill went on talking. Occasionally he would glance at her, but he didn't seem to expect her to answer. Once, when the wagon reached the crest of a small hill and they looked down into a hollow filled with colourful wild flowers, Ellen drew in her breath loudly.

"You like flowers Ellen?" Bill asked.

Ellen told him about selling nosegays at the dockside in Liverpool. That made her think of Uncle Bert and her eyes shaded over with regret.

"You want to stop and pick some?" asked Bill. She shook her head. He clicked his tongue to hurry Prince along.

The next time Bill spoke it was to point out a rough track that led to his farm. "That's the way I'd go if I was going to my place. My shack is just over that rise. You should come and see me sometime." He laughed. "I'll try to have the place tidied up a bit. It'd be a shock to you after Mum's place. See that clump of trees up ahead? That's home. Won't be long now. In a minute you'll be able to see the corner of the roof."

Ellen's stomach turned over. She sat up straight and stared at the brown peak. It disappeared as the road took a dip, but as soon as they came out of the hollow, Prince turned in at a gate and the whole farmyard lay before her. There was a whitewashed house and several other buildings and a girl picking peas in a vegetable garden. Her dog began to bark noisily. She dropped her basket and ran to the house, calling, "Mum! Hilda! Come quick! Bill's got somebody with him."

A tall man wearing a broad-brimmed straw hat stepped out of the barn and walked toward them, shushing the dog on the way.

"Hello Dad," said Bill, with a grin. "Look what I picked up for you at the station."

"Who's this then?" asked the man in a quiet, pleasant voice.

Bill jumped down and held the horse's head. "This is Miss Ellen Winter. Your orphan."

"Ah!"

"I'm not an orphan," said Ellen faintly.

"Of course you're not." Mr. Aitken reached up and swung her to the ground. A slow smile spread across his face. His pale blue eyes twinkled. "You've got a home now," he said.

By this time his daughter had returned with her sister. Mr. Aitken turned Ellen around to face them saying, "Here are May and Hilda. Girls, meet Ellen."

Ellen exchanged shy nods with the girl from the garden and then gazed up at a young lady with soft waves of brown hair framing brown eyes with long lashes.

"We've been waiting for you for so long Ellen," Hilda said and her voice was as low and pleasant as her father's. She took Ellen by the hand and led her toward the house. At the door stood a tall, thin lady with hair pulled severely into a bun. She looked at the child closely, then she smiled and her whole face was transformed. She reached out and took Ellen's trembling hands in a firm clasp. "Welcome to your new home," she said.

At supper, Ellen met the hired man, Fred Harder.

"From Liverpool, are you?" he said with delight. "It'll be a nice change to have someone on my side against all these Canadians."

"Now, Fred," said Mr. Aitken, "you've told us often

enough that you were glad to leave England."

At the time Fred left school, there was a depression in the cotton industry and jobs in the north of England were scarce. One day he answered an advertisement from Canada that promised to teach farming skills to young Englishmen so that they could farm on their own in two or three years. His relatives helped him to raise the money for the apprenticeship fee and his passage to Brandon, Manitoba.

"It was a sell-out," Fred told Ellen. "There were four of us that had signed on at the same time. Well, it didn't take us long to find out that we was paying that no-good farmer to do all his work while he lolled around having afternoon tea. He wasn't teaching us a thing. He couldn't. He didn't know anything about farming. So, one day I just walked out. Couldn't get my money back and I needed a job. I heard Mr. Aitken wanted a hired man so I came along to see him."

"And not feeling overly bright just at that moment, I hired him," said the farmer with a laugh.

"I'm learning boss, I'm learning."

"Yes, well come along and I'll teach you to mend a rail fence," said Mr. Aitken. He winked at Ellen, pushed back his chair and reached for his hat.

Fred groaned and unwound his short legs from the chair rungs. "There's one lesson I've learned and you'll learn it too Ellen. It's this—there's always work to do on a farm, plenty of work. Thanks for the food," he said to Mrs. Aitken, as he followed the farmer outside and carefully shut the screen door behind him.

Half an hour later, Ellen heard wagon wheels crunch down the drive. May rushed to the window, saying, "That's probably Sam! I wonder if he brought Prissy and.... He did! He brought Prissy and the baby!" She rushed outside.

Hilda smiled at Ellen. "She's crazy about our baby nephew. Sam's our older brother. He and Priscilla have the farm to the north of us." She broke off as May returned carrying a bundle wrapped in white mosquito netting. Several pairs of hands stripped off the netting to reveal a round-eyed, curly-haired, gurgling baby. While the three Aitkens joined in fussing over him, the baby's mother smiled warmly at Ellen.

"I'm Priscilla," she said. "Bill stopped on his way home and told us you had arrived. Welcome!"

"Yes, glad you're here," echoed Sam, from the doorway.

Even Teddy made her feel welcome by giving her a punch on the nose when May called her over to admire him.

Chapter 4

The next morning, Ellen walked two and a half miles to school with Hilda and May. Although everyone said it would be another hot day, the morning was cool and pleasant. The roadside and empty fields were covered with wildflowers like those Ellen had seen the day before. She recognized some of them: buttercups, purple daisies and wild pea. Hilda told her the names of others: yarrow, goldenrod, black-eyed susans and orange lilies. At the corner where they were to turn east, Miranda Flett and her collie dog were waiting for them. Miranda was seven years old and every morning since starting school she had walked with Hilda and May.

"Go home, Gyp! Home!" she ordered the dog and then skipped to meet them, swinging her tin lunch pail. She took Hilda's hand and walked ahead with her.

"That's the Osbornes' land over there," said May. "There's three of them at school. Florrie's eleven, like you. Then there's Michael, he's ten and David is eight, but he's still in the 'baby Reader' like Miranda."

"I can do adding better than him," Miranda called back over her shoulder.

"The Meadows' place is on this side," May went on. "The school house is on the corner of their land in the far quarter."

"Are we nearly there then?" The new boots she'd been given in Toronto had rubbed a blister on Ellen's heel. She envied Miranda's bare feet.

"Won't be long now," answered May. "Hilda boards at the Meadows' in winter so she'll be close to the school. They have three children, but only Dorothy comes to school. She's seven and real smart."

Ellen interrupted, "Why does Hilda board out in winter and not you?"

May laughed. "Oh, it doesn't matter if I can't get to school, but the teacher *has* to be there."

"But, why can't you get there?"

"Oh, heavy snowfall, or a blizzard. Once last year I couldn't go for a whole week on account of a blizzard and then Dad had to dig a path for me out to the road."

Before Ellen could ask what a blizzard was, Hilda called back, "There's the school."

Eagerly, Ellen looked past a grove of poplar trees to a one-story wooden building about the size of the Aitkens' house. The weathered boards were a pretty silvery-grey color. The girls crossed the porch into a square entry with two doors, one leading to a combined cloakroom and store-room and the other into the big schoolroom. Along the north wall, three long, narrow windows gave a view of an open field and the Meadows' house in the distance. On the back wall, low bookshelves held the textbooks plus a few well-worn volumes for students wanting to read in their spare time. A map of Canada, and another of the world with the British Empire marked in pink, hung above the bookshelves. Ellen took a deep breath. She had attended six different schools in England and they all smelled the same as this one: chalk, old books, stale air. Hilda raised the windows and left the door wide open to admit the fresh morning breeze. In a few minutes, Dorothy Meadows came running in, pigtails flying, and presented Hilda with a large bouquet of mignonette which soon perfumed the whole room.

There were six double desks in the room. "Ellen, you'll sit at the back with May. She can help you while you're getting used to things."

Dorothy and Miranda sat down in the front row and put their heads together to whisper. The other children stayed outside until Hilda rang the hand bell. David Osborne and Peter Johnson plopped into the seats in front of May. They were only little kids. Ellen wouldn't have any trouble with them. The ones across the aisle were different. Florrie Osborne looked friendly, but the other girl, Helen Barrie, had her nose in the air. Their younger brothers sat in front of them, close to the teacher's desk. When everyone else was settled, Lawrence Johnson, twelve years old, stomped in carrying a full pail of water. He placed it on a shelf near his seat in front of Ellen. He stared at her while Hilda introduced her to the class. "Another snob from England," he muttered in disgust.

During the next few days, Ellen discovered that she was far behind May in all subjects. That was to be expected since

May was two years older. But it hurt her pride to be put in the class with Florrie and Helen for arithmetic.

"It's the questions about money," she told them. "I don't know what you're talking about. What are dollars?"

The children were all sitting in the shade of the trees eating their lunch.

Lawrence said, "I knew you were just another English dummy."

He didn't really care about Ellen; he was just teasing Bradley Barrie again. The Barrie family had come out from England the year before but Bradley had not yet learned to ignore Lawrence's insults. He jumped up, upsetting the lunch pail he was sharing with his sister, and rushed at the bigger boy with fists raised. Lawrence remained seated but wrapped his arms around his head and pretended to be afraid.

"Oh, this big English bully is going to beat me up," he said in a falsetto voice.

"Dad'll beat you if you fight again, Brad," warned his sister.

"He's always making smart remarks about the English," stormed Bradley.

"Ignore him! That's what Mum says. He's just trying to get your goat. Anyway," added Helen, "she's not *our* kind of English."

Florrie, who had been helping the little girls to rinse out their milk bottles, looked up in surprise. "I didn't know there were different kinds," she said.

"What do you mean?" Ellen demanded.

"I know what you are," Helen answered mysteriously.

All the children waited for her to go on. Ellen's lunch felt like lead in her stomach.

"What is she?" asked Dorothy at last.

"She's a workhouse brat."

Ellen leaped up. "I'm not! I'm not!" she yelled.

"Yes you are. My father saw you and a boy get off the train in town. He says you were both dressed like orphans. He says you were a workhouse brat if ever he saw one."

"I'm not a workhouse brat! I've got an uncle back in Liverpool!"

Helen looked down her thin nose. "Oh yes you are," she said calmly. "You were wearing an orphan's uniform. My dad says you can always tell."

Just as Ellen reached out to swat Helen, Hilda called the children to come for a ball game. Dorothy and Miranda ran off to their playhouse in the woods. Ellen would gladly have gone with them, but Hilda insisted she learn to play 'scrub' baseball. "Come along, you'll pick it up in no time," she encouraged.

Ellen thought about Helen's remark all day. She was right about the dress. You *could* always tell. Well, she just wouldn't wear the dress or cloak ever again! She thought of Mrs. Aitken folding both carefully away in the tin trunk at the foot of the bed. "There's lots of good wear left in these," she had said. Well, I won't ever wear them, Ellen vowed. I'm not an orphan and I won't dress like one!

As soon as the two girls arrived home, they did their chores. May and her dog, John A. (he was named after the Prime Minister) went to fetch the cows. This was a job May hated and couldn't wait to turn over to Ellen as the youngest in the family. First though, John A. had to learn to obey the newcomer.

Instead, Ellen picked green beans into a bushel basket for Mrs. Aitken to preserve. As she worked, she glanced often at a fire smouldering in one corner of the vegetable patch. An idea was forming in her head. Dare she? Why not? They were her clothes. Well, not really, but the Aitkens hadn't paid for them. She should be able to do what she wanted with them. If she didn't get rid of them, Mrs. Aitken would certainly make her wear them again and then Helen would call her an orphan. By the time she carried the full basket into the kitchen she had made up her mind.

"Thanks," said Mrs. Aitken. "Now will you peel these potatoes for supper? I'll be out in the milk house for a while."

As soon as she'd gone, Ellen looked quickly around the house and yard. There was no one in sight. She ran upstairs, pulled the hated brown dress and grey woollen cape from her trunk, and hurried outside. With the clothes in a bundle under her arm, she opened the gate to the garden and ran to the fire. It was almost out. Quickly, she threw on some dry stalks to make it blaze up and then dropped the dress and cloak into the flames. With a stick, she poked at the cloth to keep it burning. No one was going to make her wear orphan's clothes! The smouldering wool began to smell. Ellen poked the fire into a blaze again. "Hurry up and burn," she muttered.

Suddenly, she heard Mrs. Aitken's voice. "Ellen! Ellen, what are you doing? You've left the gate open. Close it, please.... What's that smell? Ellen? Ellen!" She came into the garden, closing the gate herself. "What in the world are you doing?" She snatched the stick from Ellen and drew the cloak out of the fire. "Burning your clothes! Well, I never! What are you up to? Look, they're quite spoiled."

Ellen trembled as she gazed up at Mrs. Aitken's stern face. But she was glad to hear that the clothes were ruined.

"Go into the house and finish the potatoes. I'll talk to you later."

The supper table was quiet. Mrs. Aitken hung the scorched cape on the kitchen door and told everyone what Ellen had done. Her disapproval lay like a blanket over the family, but she would allow no discussion of the subject at the table. Next to her apprehension, the hardest thing for Ellen to bear was the sorrowful look that Hilda had given her.

After supper, as the Aitkens led Ellen into the parlour, Hilda said, "Mum, I think Helen Barrie was teasing Ellen at noon hour. Maybe that has something to do with what happened."

"Thank you Hilda," her mother replied sternly. "You may trust your father and me to get to the bottom of this."

In summer, the parlour was seldom used and the room seemed stuffy and formal after the cozy busyness of the kitchen. Mrs. Aitken sat at the table and motioned Ellen to stand in front of her. Mr. Aitken, looking very uncomfortable, sat on the settee, a little behind his wife. He rubbed his hand over his glistening bald head and when Ellen stole a glance at him, he gave her a tiny wink.

Mrs. Aitken went right to the point. "Why did you burn your clothes Ellen?"

Ellen was silent. How much should she explain? If she told them everything, would they send her away to another family?

"I'm waiting, Ellen." Mrs. Aitken tapped her hand on the table.

"Was it something that Helen Barrie said?" asked Mr. Aitken in his quiet voice.

Ellen nodded miserably.

"What did she say?" he asked.

"She called me a workhouse brat! She said I was an orphan!"

Surprise replaced sternness on Mrs. Aitken's face. "But you *are* an orphan," she said.

"No I'm not! I've got an uncle in England. I lived with him and I'm going to go home to Uncle Bert as soon as I can!"

"This sounds like nonsense to me," said the woman crisply. "What do you mean?"

Ellen hesitated for a moment, then she took a deep breath and began. "Well, I was selling flowers on the dock and a fire broke out and everybody ran around—to get away from the fire, like. And I jumped into a boat with some orphans. They was going to Canada, see? So the sailors pushed off and we went out to the ship and I had to go on it with the others."

"Why?"

"On account of the fire," said Ellen. She crossed and uncrossed her feet and rubbed her moist palms on her skirt.

"I see. The dock was on fire, was that it?"

"Yes."

"But why didn't they send you back?"

"They was supposed to, with the pilot, from Ireland, only there was a fog, a real pea-souper, and we couldn't land and so we—me, and the pilot—had to come on to Quebec." Ellen went on talking rapidly, explaining about Miss Fawcett taking charge of her, and about the cable and its strange reply.

When she had finished, Mr. and Mrs. Aitken looked at one another for a long minute.

"Well," said Mrs. Aitken, "that's quite a story. What do you think Wilf?"

"Poor little tyke," he said.

"Yes, if it's true."

Ellen's mouth went dry. Was the story true? She hadn't told any lies, but she had left some things out. Did that count as lying?

"Ellen, look at me."

With an effort, the girl met Mrs. Aitken's eyes. "Did you just make up an uncle because you don't like to be called an orphan?"

"No! No! You'll see! Uncle Bert will send me the money to go home."

"Don't you want to live with us, Ellen?" Mr. Aitken asked rather sadly.

Ellen hung her head. "You're kind," she said. "I like you all. But... Uncle Bert... he's my family."

Mrs. Aitken lifted Ellen's chin and looked straight into her eyes. After a minute, she said, "I believe you, child." She sighed. "It's a bad mix-up and I don't quite see what to do about it. Someone from the Orphan Society will be coming to make a report in the next few months. We'll tell her then. In the meantime, I suppose we'll have to try and get in touch with your uncle. You'll have to stay here, at least until we hear from him."

"Ellen could write to him on Sunday, Charlotte. Let him know where she is."

"Yes, you could do that Ellen. But what you did was

wrong and you'll have to be punished. There's no excuse for destroying perfectly good clothes."

Her husband rubbed his head again. "Well now Charlotte, you can understand why the child objected to being called a workhouse brat."

"Leave this to me please, Wilf. I'll think of a punishment."

"You can beat me if you want to," Ellen said bravely.

"No no," said Mr. Aitken, much distressed.

"I won't beat you Ellen. Don't talk nonsense. I should make you wear the cloak." Ellen felt the blood drain from her face. "But it's too badly scorched. Can you sew?"

"Yes Ma'am."

"You will cut the cloak down and make a small one out of it. Someone will make use of it. And you must do it all by yourself."

"Yes Ma'am, I will." Ellen was relieved. She didn't care who wore the cloak as long as she didn't have to.

Fred was still sitting with Hilda and May in the kitchen and they all looked up eagerly when the three returned. Once again, Ellen told the story of her adventures. Hilda offered to help her write the letter to Uncle Bert.

In bed that night, May told Ellen not to let Helen Barrie bother her. "She's always trying to make trouble. But listen, are you really going to go back to England?"

"Yes, as soon as Uncle Bert sends me the money."

May sighed. "And I thought I was going to get out of fetching the cows."

Ellen giggled. "It will likely be a long time before he saves enough money," she said.

Chapter 5

As Fred had predicted, there was plenty of work on the farm. And though Ellen was used to working for her living, she was not used to the hard physical labor of bringing in pails of clean water from the well or the rain barrel and carrying dirty water out. The wood box beside the stove also had to be kept full. Ellen had to help with washing clothes, scrubbing floors, dusting furniture and cleaning sooty lamp chimneys. The vegetable garden had to be weeded and watered and the produce picked and preserved. One Saturday morning she went with May on the last blueberry picking expedition of the season.

When they brought in the berries, Mrs. Aitken said, "Now, Ellen, you can make them into a pie."

Ellen looked at her blankly. "I don't know how."

"Can't make a pie?" exclaimed the woman. "What *can* you bake?"

"Nothing Ma'am. I never had to," answered Ellen.

"What? Past eleven years old and you can't bake! Why, May has been making bread since she was ten." She opened the big flour bin. "You must be able to bake bread. You will have your first lesson right now."

So, in addition to all her other chores, Ellen learned to make bread. She was very proud when one of her loaves was considered good enough to give to Bill. Her first pie was a failure, but the pigs ate it happily. The second was a bit better. Mr. Aitken and Fred both praised it, even though they said "no thanks" to a second piece.

Ellen was determined and she tried again and again. One day the school inspector came to dinner. After finishing his third piece of pie he leaned back and patted his fat stomach.

"You still make the best pie in Onala District Mrs. Aitken. Nobody to touch you," he said.

Mrs. Aitken smiled. "I'm glad you liked it, but I didn't make it," she answered.

"What?" he exclaimed. "Young May that good a cook already! Better look out!"

"Good for you May," said her father.

May was careful not to look at Ellen who was standing behind the inspector ready to serve him more tea. She said, "I didn't make it."

Ellen was trying so hard not to laugh out loud that she almost poured the hot tea on the visitor.

Mr. Aitken looked bewildered. "Then who... ?" He stared wide-eyed at the two grinning girls. "Not Ellen! Was that one of Ellen's pies? Well, you surely have a quick pupil Charlotte."

"Your uncle's going to be glad to get you back," said Fred. "Bet he's never tasted a pie like that!"

Ellen nearly burst with pride.

She was not such a success at learning to milk. The cows frightened her. So did the horse. The pigs, Fred's special charge, were easier to deal with. For one thing, they always stayed in their own sty.

Mrs. Aitken put her in charge of the poultry—ten Leghorn hens and a rooster. She had to feed them, gather the eggs, keep the chicken coop clean and lock the hens in at night. This last was a very important task because skunks and mink were always looking for a feast of eggs, and coyotes, who lived in the hills to the west, were noted chicken thieves.

One night Ellen was awakened by howling coyotes. She lay beside May, who slept peacefully, and listened to the frightening sound of their call. Pulling the covers up closely around her neck, she snuggled down into the comfort of the bed, but she couldn't fall asleep again.

Why did she wake tonight? She should be used to their howling. She shivered slightly. They couldn't get at the hens. The door was locked. Suddenly, she had a vision of herself standing at the door of the low henhouse waiting for the last bird to enter. Hilda and May had called her to hurry because they were going to pick some bluebells before it got dark. She remembered that one hen had skittered off instead of going in. She also remembered chasing and catching it, only to find that two more had wandered out. She had chased them back too, thrown the first one in and slammed the door. But, had she locked it?

She closed her eyes tight and concentrated as she went over the scene. She must have locked the door! The coyotes howled again. That was certainly nearer. Then John A.

barked. That settled it. John A. never bothered barking when they were off in the hills. Although she had never seen a coyote, she pictured a wolf-like animal sneaking up to the henhouse, finding the door unlocked and pushing his way in. He couldn't. John A. would chase him away. Then she heard the dog bark again off in the distance. Sweat beaded her upper lip. She wiped it off with the sheet.

Fred had told her that coyotes were very intelligent. "One or two will lure a guard dog away while another kills a chicken and carries it off. Then they meet back at their den and share the spoils. Smart! You have to remember to lock that henhouse door or they'll get all them dumb birds."

Suppose that was happening now? Mrs. Aitken would be mad if all her hens were lost. And Mr. Aitken and Hilda would be awfully disappointed in her. They all trusted her to do the job right. She must go and make sure the door was locked.

Carefully, she pushed back the covers and slid out of bed. She must not wake May. None of the family must know if she had forgotten to lock the door. With outstretched hands she felt her way to the hall. A floorboard creaked. No one stirred. Her bare feet made no sound as she glided toward the enclosed stairwell. The door at the bottom was shut. She hesitated a few moments before stepping down into the black tunnel. The stairway was steep and long. She began to wonder whether she was dreaming—one of those terrible dreams when you seem to be walking and walking and never arriving at your destination. Then she bumped into the door. She gasped and almost ran upstairs again.

"No," she whispered sternly to herself. "You have to go and lock the door."

"But I'm sure I did," her scared self answered.

"No, you're not sure, or you wouldn't be here. Now, lift that latch."

Fred slept in a little room at the foot of the stairs so, if there was anything frightening in the kitchen, she could call him.

After the closeness of the stairwell, the kitchen felt open and airy but she could still see nothing. On tiptoe, she groped her way past chairs and table and washstand, stubbing her toe only once. Then she was outside on the low stoop. Her heart beat quickly as she paused to look around. There was no moon, but by the pale starlight she could make out the shape of the barn and the pigsty next to it. In daylight, she would have walked straight ahead across the yard, through the gate and alongside the barn to the henhouse a few yards beyond it to the right. But she knew she didn't have the courage to walk past the barn in the dark. Something... anything... could be lurking in those shadows. Holding her breath, she peered intently toward the henhouse. Was the door swinging open? She listened. No sound came from nearby, but far off in the hills a coyote howled again and a dog barked. That was a good sign! It probably meant there was no coyote in the yard. The hens would be safe tonight, and she wouldn't ever forget to lock the door again.

She remembered Mr. Aitken saying, "Don't ever forget to lock the door, Ellen. Charlotte sets great store by her hens. She's got the best layers in the district and she's proud of them. Chickens are hard to keep around here. They've got so many enemies. You have to be awful watchful."

"I won't forget, " Ellen had promised.

Remembering this, she walked firmly across the side yard
and into the vegetable garden, being careful to close the
gate behind her. Then she began to wish that she had taken
the route past the barn. Many of the plants were dying and
the dry stalks rustled menacingly as she crept down the rows.

Quickly, she scrambled over the rail fence and stood
panting on the other side. Now the henhouse was just yards
away. It was so quiet that she was sure there could be no wild
animal around. Or had the hens already been eaten? The
back corner of the building had an odd curve in it. She
couldn't remember anything that shape. She got goose
bumps. Her feet seemed rooted to the earth. She couldn't
move. Then she realized that to return to the house she
would have to turn her back on whatever was out there and
climb over the fence. Her white nightgown would make an
easy target. She took two steps forward. A black shape
detached itself from the shadow of the coop and streaked
away across the field.

Blood rushed to Ellen's head and her hands tingled. "Try
to kill my chickens will you?" she exclaimed aloud. She ran
to the henhouse and felt along the edge of the closed door.
The toggle was hanging free! She had not locked the door!
Yanking it open, she peered inside. Eleven dim shapes lined
the roost. All safe! Ellen rammed the toggle into the lock and
then turned and raced for the house and the safety of bed.

In the morning, May noticed how tired John A. was.

"He must have been chasing something in the night,"
she said. "Rabbits, do you think? Or coyotes?"

"Coyotes!" exclaimed her mother. "Oh, the brutes! Ellen
don't ever forget to lock the henhouse door, will you?"

"No, I won't," replied Ellen, without looking up.

Taking care of the chickens, helping in the house and garden, learning to bake, going to school—the chores were endless. Sometimes Ellen wanted to hide in the poplar bluff, surrounded by trees, where no one could find her to remind her of another task. She longed to sit and daydream about her reunion with Uncle Bert.

But at harvest time, there was certainly no time for daydreaming! The work of the farm doubled. School closed at the end of September so that the children could help with bringing in the wheat. The boys worked with the men to cut and stook the grain and then, after it was threshed, filled the grain bags. The girls and women took over the men's regular chores and cooked huge meals for the threshing crew.

Two years before, the farmers of Onala District had joined together to buy a steam thresher. A gang of men went with the machine from farm to farm until all the wheat was in bags and stored in granaries. Lawrence's father was the boss of the gang and Sam Aitken was the engineer in charge of the machine.

"The engineer is the most important man on the whole gang," May boasted to Ellen. "If he can't keep the machine going, no one can work."

The gang was made up of four men who were hired by the day. Lawrence was bag boy. At each farm the farmer and his family helped. To Ellen it seemed that harvest time was a race with winter. If the weather remained good and the thresher didn't break down too often, the farmers would get in their crop before the snow fell.

It was a Monday morning when the gang moved into the

Aitken barn which was to be their bunkhouse while they threshed for Mr. Aitken, Sam and Bill. For the next week, Mrs. Aitken, Hilda, Prissy, May and Ellen worked harder than Ellen had ever seen anyone work in her life. Everyone seemed to know exactly what to do. No one had time to teach the new girl anything. So, Ellen found herself doing lots of jobs that required little skill. She swept floors, carried in endless armloads of wood and buckets of water, watched over baby Teddy, cut up vegetables, set tables and cleared them off, and carried mid-morning and afternoon tea to the men in the field. She didn't mind that too much because she could take a few minutes to rest while the men did.

It was on one of these breaks that Fred introduced her to Jimmy Castle.

"Here's someone you should meet Ellen," said Fred. "This skinny fellow under all the dust is a countryman of ours. Jimmy Castle. Comes from Liverpool, same as you."

"Really?" asked Ellen with an eager smile.

Lawrence was standing nearby, helping himself from the water pail Ellen had brought out. He wiped his arm across his mouth, leaving black streaks on nose and chin. He laughed loudly. "Riley?" he mimicked. "Cor, blimey, you limeys sure talk funny!"

Ellen reddened and frowned.

Fred merely said in a kindly tone, "Run away and take care of your bags."

"Limeys!" sneered Lawrence. "Three limeys!"

The steam whistle blew to end the rest period.

"I'd like a natter about the old home town," Jimmy said as he heaved himself up from the stubble. "I'll see you after we quit for the day, will I?"

But the work day did not end till the sun had set and Mrs. Aitken would not allow Ellen to go out to the barn where the men slept. "That's no place for a young lady," she said.

The next day, however, the steam engine broke down for the third time. Sam tinkered with it for several minutes, but finally decided he must go to town for a new part. The men had an enforced rest of several hours. But not the women, as the men had to be fed whether they worked or not.

In the afternoon, when she had finished peeling and quartering a bucketful of potatoes, Ellen slipped out before Mrs. Aitken could give her another job. The barn door was ajar and Ellen stepped inside. Straw beds had been placed in one corner and the men sprawled on them enjoying the unexpected holiday. Two were playing cards. Lawrence was whittling. Jimmy Castle was sitting on a bale of hay playing the mouth organ while Fred listened, tapping his toes and humming off key. The tune was a sentimental music hall ballad that Ellen had heard before.

"Uncle Bert used to play that," she said, stepping boldly forward.

"And who's Uncle Bert?" asked Jimmy.

Fred laughed. "A bloke we hear a lot about," he answered.

"Herbert Winter," answered Ellen. She was a little hurt by Fred's laughter. "He's the best violinist in the world. He plays the flute too. He plays in the Princess Theatre all the time and he's played in the Royal Concert Hall lots of times."

"Has he?" said Jimmy. "I've played there a time or two myself, when they needed an extra trombone. Herbert Winter you say?"

Ellen clasped her hands and teetered forward on her toes. "Do you know him?" she asked eagerly.

"Little short fellow? Kind of sandy hair? Full of jokes?"

"Yes! Yes, you know him!" Ellen looked triumphantly at Fred.

Fred grinned and shrugged his shoulders.

Jimmy tilted his head to the side and gazed at Ellen. "I know you too," he said.

"Do you? I don't remember you."

"Remember the Priestleys? Used to have big parties with lots of people and plenty of music? Musical 'sworays', Mrs. P. used to call 'em."

"Yes! The Priestleys are friends of ours. We've gone there lots of times."

"Well, I only went a couple of times, but one time Herbert Winter was there with his little girl. He played and she sang. Was that you?"

Ellen nodded.

"You still sing?"

Ellen shook her head.

"Why not? You had a lovely voice. Everyone said so."

"I'd like to hear you sing Ellen," said Fred.

"What songs do you know?" asked Jimmy.

Ellen rubbed her nose and sniffed. "I know the one you were playing, 'My Mother's Rose Garden'."

"Right," said Jimmy, cupping the mouth organ in his hands. "Let's have that."

Ellen started softly with many glances toward the other men, but soon she forgot where she was and let her voice soar. For a few seconds after they had finished the song there was silence in the barn. Jimmy winked at Ellen and she smiled back. The card players had stopped their game to listen. One of them said, "That was beautiful. Give us another."

Jimmy began to play 'Bobby Shaftoe.' When Ellen seemed unsure of the words, Fred supplied them so that all three smiled broadly at the end of the song.

"My word girl, you can sing!" said Fred.

"I told you!" declared Jimmy.

He played a comic song which had been a favorite of Uncle Bert's and Ellen laughed to herself as she sang it. As the impromptu concert went on, Ellen realized she was happier than she'd been since leaving England. It was almost like being home.

Just as they finished one song, the barn door was pulled fully open and Mr. Aitken stepped in. "You're wanted up at the house Ellen," he said.

Ellen stared at him in dismay. She hadn't meant to stay so long. As she slid past him, she wondered if Mrs. Aitken was very angry.

Hilda held the kitchen door open for her. "We could hear you up here Ellen. You have a lovely voice."

"That's as may be," said her mother, "but Ellen had no business going to the barn. I thought you understood me yesterday Ellen. The men's sleeping quarters are no place for a lady. Is that clear?"

"Yes Ma'am," answered Ellen.

"Finish setting the table. May has done most of your work."

Ellen couldn't read May's expression as she took the stack of dishes from her. She looked almost pleased that Ellen had been scolded and yet there was respect, too.

"When harvest is over," Hilda said, "we'll have plenty of time for music. May sings nicely too. You two might sing duets."

So May was jealous! Ellen had had that same feeling once when Uncle Bert had asked another girl to sing instead.

During that winter, they had many happy evenings around the organ in the parlour. Ellen's voice was much praised by the family and by the congregation that gathered in the schoolhouse for church each month. She was flattered, but she was even more satisfied that Jimmy Castle's visit had proved to them all that Uncle Bert really existed.

"He'll have your letter soon," Mr. Aitken said. "We can't make any plans to send you back till we hear from him, now can we? Just be patient. What can't be cured must be endured, as the man said."

Chapter 6

After the harvest was safely in the family prepared for the long winter ahead. Hilda moved to the Meadows' house on the first Sunday of November. On Fridays she walked home with the girls and stayed until Monday morning.

On her second weekend home, Hilda asked her dad if he was planning to go to town soon. "I'd like to talk to the principal of the town school," she said.

"Well," her father answered, "there's the grain to go to the elevator. Fred could take a few bags in tomorrow if you don't mind riding in the wagon."

"May I go too Mum?" asked May.

Ellen's eyes brightened. Would she be invited? She hadn't been back to the town since she arrived on the train in August.

Mrs. Aitken looked from one to the other of the questioning faces turned toward her. "You've all worked hard lately," she said. "You deserve a holiday. Yes, you may go. Ellen too."

Although snow had fallen three or four times, there was
not enough on the ground to skid a sleigh so the wagon box
was still mounted on wheels. Using the grain bags for a backrest, the three girls tucked themselves in against the frosty
air with buffalo robes and old quilts. Mr. Aitken had given
May and Ellen each five cents to spend, saying with a wink,
"That's twice as much as you deserve and half of what you're
worth." They spent most of the journey trying to decide
whether to spend their money separately or to combine it.
Four cents would buy a lot of candy and they would each
have three cents left to spend on something else. They still
had not made up their minds when they saw the town from
the top of the hill.

The Little Turtle River, now frozen almost across, flowed
through the valley at right angles to the road. Beside the
river ran the railroad. Ellen saw the small, dull-red station
where she and George had arrived and the grain elevator
where Fred would sell the wheat. Most of the town lay on the
other side of the river. Saturday was a busy day in Patterson
and there were a number of buggies and wagons on Main
Street. Ellen giggled when May exclaimed at the crowds.
"Call this busy? You should see Liverpool," she said.

Fred pulled Prince up and let the girls out at the bridge
before he turned to join the line-up of wagons at the grain
elevator. A weathered sign on the post read:

CAUTION!
CROSS AT YOUR OWN RISK
LOADED WAGONS FORBIDDEN
WALK YOUR HORSES

"Isn't the bridge safe?" asked Ellen a little fearfully as a horse trotted past them making the boards tremble.

"It's perfectly safe for people walking," said May.

On the other side of the bridge Hilda said, "You two go along to the stores. I'm going up the hill to Mr. Beatty's house. I'll meet you at the General Store later. Are you going to the Post Office first?"

"Yes!" said both girls together.

Ellen couldn't understand why Uncle Bert had not replied to her letter. Even if he couldn't send the money yet, he could have written. She raced May to a tiny store that sold baked goods and candy and had the post office in one corner. Ellen held her breath while May asked for the mail. If there was a letter from Uncle Bert, the day would be perfect. But there was no such thing. Swallowing her disappointment, she turned to the candy display. There were fruit drops, barley sugar sticks, jellies and a large piece of English treacle toffee.

"Oh!" breathed Ellen. "Toffee! Just like home!"

"Is it good?" asked May.

Ellen rolled her eyes.

"Four cents worth please," said May.

The postmistress chopped off a large chunk with a little wooden hammer and then, at May's request, broke off two small pieces. They each popped a piece in their mouths and the rest they saved to be shared with the family. They looked into every store on the street. May spent her three cents on two pencils and a scribbler, but Ellen couldn't make up her mind what to buy.

"You'll find something in here," May assured her as they

turned into the PATTERSON EMPORIUM, J. D. OLIVER, PROPRIETOR, DRY GOODS AND CHINA.

Just inside the door on an odds and ends table was a little china kitten. It was two inches high, orange and brown in colour, with bright blue eyes and pointed ears. It sat on a blue china cushion with its tail curled around its tiny paws. The tip of one ear was chipped off so it was marked down to three cents.

"It's just like a little kitten I used to play with at home," exclaimed Ellen. "Come to think of it, I've never even seen a cat out here."

"No, you won't," said May. "Cats are scarce in the west. We used to have one in Ontario. But you can't cuddle a china kitten."

"I don't care," answered Ellen. She paid for the ornament and placed it carefully in her pocket.

May had to match some wool for her mother. Mr. Oliver led her to some bins on the back wall of the store and helped her choose. Meanwhile Ellen inspected a table full of crochet cotton. The cotton, in white and two shades of beige, was displayed in the middle of the table. Around it were open boxes full of steel knitting needles, steel crochet hooks and one tatting shuttle by itself in a fairly large box. Once, Ellen and Uncle Bert had boarded with a seamstress in Liverpool. To pay for the room Ellen helped the woman with her work. She had learned to make lace both by crocheting and tatting. At the time it had seemed a tedious chore, but compared to the coarse, black stockings Mrs. Aitken was making her knit, the lace-making seemed pleasant. Ellen picked up the tatting shuttle now and dreamed of home.

Her daydream was shattered by a tapping sound. A woman leaned out of a buggy and rapped on the front show window with the butt end of her whip.

"Samuel!" called Mr. Oliver.

A freckled face poked out of a door almost beside Ellen, startling her.

"Sir?" said the boy.

"Go and hold Mrs. Dundonald's horse! Be quick!"

Samuel put on a toque and struggled into an overcoat. Ellen leaned against the table to let him go by.

"Scamper, boy! Don't keep Mrs. Dundonald waiting!" said the storekeeper. He hurried to hold the door open. A proud-looking woman swept in. She wore a brown cloth coat with a sable fur collar, a tall sable hat and a large muff to match.

"I'm in a hurry, Mr. Oliver. You know my horse is nervous and doesn't like to stand." She gestured with her muff to the back of the store. "I want to look at the crochet cotton."

Ellen replaced the tatting shuttle and started toward the door, but Mrs. Dundonald and the storekeeper bore down upon her. She was forced to back up behind the table. The space on the other side was so small that if she tried to squeeze through she would push the table against the woman, so she waited quietly where she was. After a brief look, Mrs. Dundonald ignored her.

"I want to start some new work tonight. Do you have a tatting shuttle? I gave mine to my daughter. Is that the last one? Well, I'll take it. Let me see the cotton." She laid her muff down on the counter, pulled off her gloves and picked up a ball of white cotton. She drew a length of it through her fingers, then put it down and picked up two beige balls and compared colors.

Ellen glanced at May, who raised her eyebrows very high and pantomimed examining a ball of cotton. Ellen looked down at her boots to hide a smile.

Finally the lady made up her mind. "Eight balls of the darker beige, then," she said.

Mr. Oliver gathered up the balls of cotton and carried them up to the front counter. Mrs. Dundonald picked up her muff and gloves and followed. Ellen joined the end of the procession and slipped between the lady and two other customers to stand beside May.

"And the tatting shuttle Mr. Oliver. Did you get that?"

"I will in a moment Mrs. Dundonald." He walked back to the table and looked in the box. "Did you pick it up Mrs. Dundonald?" he asked.

"No!"

"It's not in the box. Are you sure... ?"

"I did not!" said Mrs. Dundonald.

Ellen and May, having finished buttoning their coats and pulling on mittens, turned to the door.

"Just a moment!" said the lady in a loud voice. "Girl! You were beside the table. Did you see the shuttle?"

"I put it back in the box," answered Ellen.

"Then where is it?" Mrs. Dundonald asked coldly.

"Maybe it fell on the floor," May answered.

"No, it's not on the floor," Mr. Oliver said. "And not between the boxes. Or in the wrong box." He went on looking all over the table. "Well, that's funny. It's just vanished."

"Not funny at all Mr. Oliver. The girl obviously stole it."

Ellen's stomach knotted.

"She didn't!" May exclaimed indignantly. "Ellen wouldn't steal!"

"Indeed?" said Mrs. Dundonald. "Who is she anyway?"

Mr. Oliver looked distressed. "I'm sure the girl didn't take it Mrs. Dundonald. That's Wilf Aitken's girl, May, and the Home Child they've taken in."

"A Home Child! Well, no wonder!" Mrs. Dundonald was furious. "If that isn't just like Charlotte Aitken! Taking in a Home Child! Those children are England's garbage! Gutter sweepings! Swept up and shipped over here for us to deal with. I've no patience for that." She turned to one of the other customers. "You remember back in Ontario, Mrs. Bastow, it was Annie Macpherson bringing in thousands of them. And Dr. Barnardo!"

"Aye, and he's going to set up a Home and Farm out here in the west," answered Mrs. Bastow.

"We saw to it that it wouldn't be anywhere near Patterson," declared Mrs. Dundonald. "We don't want any part of that! Just criminals, the lot of them. Everyone knows those children are thieves."

"Ellen's not... " began May, but there was no stopping the angry woman.

"She was holding the shuttle when I came in," she declared.

May looked at Mr. Oliver and the other two ladies, but she could see that they were not going to help. "I'm going to get my sister," she said. "Wait here!" May dashed out.

"Shall we wait for Hilda Aitken, Mrs. Dundonald?" asked the storekeeper nervously. "She'll be able to recover the shuttle if the girl took it."

"I haven't all day to stand around here. You can see that your boy is having trouble holding my horse." She tapped her foot impatiently.

The storekeeper looked more anxious than ever. Mrs. Dundonald was an important woman in town. But the Aitkens were good customers too. And there was no proof against the child. The unhappy man went back to the table and began to search again among the boxes.

It seemed that May had been gone a very long time. What if she and Hilda believed that Ellen was a thief and didn't come back at all? The ladies went on talking about English orphans, Mrs. Dundonald staring at Ellen contemptuously the whole time.

Suddenly, the angry woman burst out, "She should be locked up!"

Ellen shuddered. Locked up! Jail! All at once the scene on the dock at Liverpool came back to her. Why were people always calling her a thief? She wasn't! Yet awful things happened to her when people accused her. Last time she had lost Uncle Bert. Would she lose the Aitkens too? She stared about her in horror. Mr. Oliver's worried frown seemed to turn into a malicious leer. Mrs. Dundonald appeared to be ten feet tall. Ellen turned and fled.

She dashed out the door, slamming it behind her. She looked to the right. Two men stood talking, blocking the sidewalk. To the left, a stern-faced woman was approaching. Mrs. Dundonald's buggy cut her off from the road, but she might be able to scamper across the seat and drop down on the other side.

She climbed onto the small iron step and flung herself

into the buggy. Suddenly, she was jerked off her feet as the vehicle began to move.

Samuel would rather not have held Mrs. Dundonald's horse. He knew it to be a nervous animal that would bolt at any sudden noise or movement. When May ran from the store, it shied, but as she ran in the opposite direction Samuel was able to quiet him. When Ellen burst out of the door and leapt into the buggy, however, Samuel was so startled that he dropped the lead rein. The horse, feeling the jolt as someone entered the buggy and realizing that his head was free, began to move quickly. Ellen was thrown back on to the seat with a bump. This further startled the horse and he reared up and trotted fast. Samuel shouted. The storekeeper and Mrs. Dundonald reached the sidewalk in time to see Ellen riding off in the buggy. Both of them began to scold loudly; she at Ellen and he at Samuel. People who saw what was happening added to the din by shouting at one another to "Get out of the way" or "Stop that horse!" Soon the horse was bolting. He pounded down the street with the buggy swaying and pitching behind him.

Ellen was terrified. After the first few moments, she grabbed one of the bars which held up the canopy. As long as the buggy remained upright, she was in no danger of being thrown out. But she had no means of controlling the horse. The reins, which had been loosely knotted around the cross bar, had worked free and were now flapping against the animal's side well out of her reach. Her heart was pounding loudly. She could see people scurrying out of the way and horses being turned to avoid the runaway. Now the bolting horse was fast approaching the bridge. All Ellen could think of was the sign she had noticed when Fred let them out of the wagon. CROSS AT YOUR OWN RISK! WALK YOUR HORSES! If they hit the bridge at this pace, it might collapse and she'd either be killed in the wreck or drowned.

So far, she hadn't uttered a sound, but she almost let out a scream when she saw two men, instead of getting out of the way, move into her path and block the entrance to the bridge. One of them had the brightest red beard Ellen had ever seen. She gasped as he climbed the bridge railing and stood on the narrow top board. At the last possible moment, the other man leapt out of the way. Checking only slightly, the horse thundered onto the bridge. The buggy wheels caught momentarily on the first board and Ellen's head smacked soundly into the hard leather backrest. She was only vaguely aware that the man on the railing jumped into the buggy as it passed. He landed on his shoulder. The frightened horse ran faster than ever and they fairly flew over the bridge. Fred, who was watching open-mouthed on the other side of the river, said afterwards that the reason the bridge didn't collapse was that the horse and buggy barely touched it. Through a haze, Ellen watched the young man right himself and grab the flapping reins. He pulled hard on them and finally gained control of the horse. But he couldn't stop him. The horse ran for another quarter of a mile, trotted for several more minutes and finally slowed to a reasonable pace. The young man turned him in a wide arc on a stretch of hard earth and headed him back to town.

By this time, Ellen had caught her breath and she was able to murmur a thanks to her rescuer.

He turned to her with an anxious look. "You all right?" he asked.

She nodded and winced at the pain in her head.

He grinned. "Your head and my shoulder. This animal has a lot to answer for."

The buggy rumbled back over the bridge. On the sidewalk in front of the Emporium stood May, Hilda, the storekeeper, Mrs. Dundonald and Samuel as well as several other curious people. All of them looked very serious. Were they going to put her in jail?

A man from the livery stable caught the horse's head. "Well done, Rudy!" he called to Ellen's rescuer. Then he turned to the horse. "Poor boy! Poor boy!" he murmured as he rubbed the animal's nose.

Rudy jumped down and was surrounded by men and boys shaking his hand and patting him on the back.

He ducked away, laughing. "Ouch! Watch my shoulder."

"Are you hurt Ellen?" Hilda asked, as she helped her climb down.

"No, I don't think so," answered Ellen in a weak voice.

Hilda gave her a fierce hug and Ellen raised her hands to her head and moaned.

Mrs. Dundonald had been busy with the stable man, ordering him to take charge of the horse, see whether he was injured and rub him down. Now she turned her attention to Ellen.

"You deserve more than a sore head!" she said. "Trying to steal my buggy!"

Hilda had listened to Mrs. Dundonald's opinion of Ellen for quite a few minutes while they all waited for the buggy to return. She now turned on the woman angrily.

"Nonsense Mrs. Dundonald!" she said. "Ellen was not trying to steal your buggy! It was an accident."

The woman's eyebrows almost touched her fur hat. "An accident was it?" She waved her muff in the air. "I saw her run out of the store. I saw her jump into the buggy. I saw her drive the horse away."

"Well, that's more than anyone else saw!" declared Hilda. "The animal ran away with Ellen!"

"And she was running away from me!"

"No wonder! You accused her of stealing and frightened her! Ellen isn't a thief." Hilda put her hand gently on the girl's arm.

"Then where's the tatting shuttle may I ask?" Mrs. Dundonald's voice was icy. "These people know she took it!" She made a wide sweep with her muff to take in the store-keeper and the spectators.

"Look!" cried May.

Everyone's eyes followed her pointing finger to Mrs. Dundonald's muff. With a puzzled frown, the woman raised and turned it. From one corner dangled the tatting shuttle. Its hook was firmly caught in a tuft of fur.

Ellen sagged against Hilda, who stared triumphantly at Mrs. Dundonald.

The woman pulled the shuttle free. "It must have caught there when I put down my muff," she said calmly. "Wrap it up with my cotton Mr. Oliver. And you'd better watch that child in the future."

"Is that all she's going to say?" gasped May. Her face reddened and she took a step forward.

"Hilda could we please leave?" Ellen begged in a trembling voice.

After a quick glance at her, Hilda said, "Yes of course. Come May, there's no use expecting any more from her. Let's find Fred and see if he's ready to go home."

As she spoke, she linked arms with both girls and led them away from the store. They had gone only a few paces when Hilda said, "Look! There's Rudy Ferguson, the man who saved you! Mr. Ferguson!"

The young man crossed the street and raised his hat to them, revealing hair as red as his beard. Cutting short Hilda's thanks, he said he would like to hear how it all happened. "Would you step into the hotel dining room and have tea and biscuits with me? I'd be greatly honored," he said, with a wink at Ellen and May.

May was thrilled with the invitation. Hilda hesitated because she knew her mother would not approve of the younger girls entering the hotel, but another look at Ellen's white face made her decide to accept.

The tea did Ellen good. After the second cup, she stopped trembling and was able to pay attention to what the others were saying. Hilda and May told Rudy he was a hero.

"We were all pretty brave," he said. "Ellen never made a sound through the whole frightening ride. And I certainly admired the way you stood up to Mrs. Dundonald, Miss Aitken. She scares me witless!"

Ellen agreed. Hilda was wonderful! Rudy had perhaps saved her life, but it was Hilda who made Ellen feel safe and secure. Still, she was not really comfortable until they were on their way home again and it was several weeks before she

could rid her mind of the words 'Home Child' and 'gutter
sweepings.' She didn't even have the pretty china kitten to
comfort her. It had been smashed to pieces in her pocket
during the wild ride.

Chapter 7

Around the beginning of December, everyone began to think about Christmas. Ellen felt very sad that she would not be spending the day with Uncle Bert. It seemed, though, that Christmas on the farm would be a more exciting time than it had been at home in England. Hilda planned a school concert for the afternoon of Christmas Eve. Everyone in the district would be invited and afterwards there would be cake and tea. May was going to read "The Cratchits' Christmas Dinner" from *A Christmas Carol* as she did every year. She was also teaching the four smallest children a choral reading about the Christmas star. Ellen had been asked to sing her favorite carol, "Silent Night." Florrie and Helen had each chosen one of the poems in the Reader to recite. Lawrence flatly refused to perform in any way. At first Michael and Bradley thought they wouldn't either.

"Well," said Hilda, "that's up to you, but you know the rule: no recitation, no dessert. My mother will be bringing a big chocolate cake."

"We'll do it!" they agreed.

At home, the family planned a party for Christmas Day. Bill, Sam, Prissy and Teddy would come, of course. The two Ransome boys, who homesteaded together nearby, were also invited. When Ellen and May delivered the bread one Monday morning, they took them the invitation.

"That'll be some Christmas present," said the elder. "Not having to eat Dale's cooking for once."

"It'll be some present not having to do the cooking!" said Dale.

Mrs. Aitken always gave the parlour walls a fresh coat of whitewash for Christmas. This year, she decided to do it while her husband and Fred were away overnight getting wood from the forest near Clear Lake. The men would cut wood all day, spend the night in a little shack, cut more wood in the morning and be back with a full sleigh by suppertime on Saturday.

When Hilda and the two younger girls arrived home that Friday afternoon, they found the parlour walls clean and bare.

"Oh good!" exclaimed May. "We can have new pictures!"

She dragged out the back issues of the *Illustrated News* and the three girls spent a happy evening cutting out pictures and pasting them on the walls.

Next morning, while the girls did the house and barn chores, Mrs. Aitken washed both pairs of hand-knit lace curtains from the parlour. It took all four of them to stretch the wet curtains onto their wooden frames.

"Careful! Don't tear it! Ease it over gently."

As each curtain was finished, it was carried outside and placed on the snow where it soon froze. When the four frames were laid out, Ellen and Hilda stood looking at them. The sun was bright, though not very warm, and it sparkled on the fresh snow that had fallen during the night.

"Look at the shadows!" said Ellen, in delight. "Every curtain is double!"

Next, Ellen carried out the braided parlour rugs and spread them flat, well away from the curtains. With a broom, she brushed fresh, clean snow onto the rugs until they were completely covered. Then she brushed them off, taking the dirt with the snow.

May came out into the yard with the velvet runner from the top of the organ, the plush table cloth and the head rest from the rocking chair and began to shake them vigorously.

"This is the way we do our work..." she sang to the tune of 'Here We Go Round the Mulberry Bush.'

Ellen laughed and joined in, brushing faster as she sang.

May carried her load inside and came out again to help Ellen fold the mats. As they stood with the long rug between them ready to fold it in half, they heard John A. barking loudly.

"What's he found I wonder?" said May. "A rabbit?"

They paused to listen. John A.'s bark became more frantic as he came closer. A grey rabbit shot through the gate and under the arch made by the rug the girls were holding. It bounded over one of the frozen curtains and disappeared around the corner of the house. The dog was hard on its heels.

"No, John A.! Don't step on the curtain," yelled May. She dropped her end of the rug and made a lunge for him, but she was too late. The dog, being heavier than the rabbit, did not bounce so lightly over the lace. Near the far edge one of his back paws went through a hole in the pattern. For a few feet, he dragged the frame with him.

May shouted again. "Stop, you dumb dog!"

Before she could reach him, he managed to shake free and go on after his quarry. Unfortunately, a thread had caught on his toenail and he pulled a large hole in the net.

May stood looking down in horror at the ruined curtain. Mum and Hilda had come to the door to investigate the noise. Still holding her end of the rug, Ellen watched the angry look spread over Mrs. Aitken's face. She was glad John A. wasn't her dog. Poor May!

When the curtains were dry and off their frames, Mrs. Aitken sat fingering the torn panel.

"What am I going to do?" she asked. "I haven't any spare cotton to mend this. And it would look terrible if I just drew it up. It's such a big hole! Drat that dog!"

"Could you cut it off above the tear and make it shorter?" asked May.

"Maybe. But I haven't time to do it before Christmas with everything else there is to do. You should do it, since he's your dog. I wish I'd taught you to knit lace."

May looked so unhappy that Ellen felt sorry for her.

"If you have a crochet hook, I can fix it," she offered. "See, I could unravel the bottom to here." She pointed to a place just above the hole. "Then I could crochet a new edge with the ravelled cotton."

Mrs. Aitken looked doubtful. "Then it would be shorter than the other three."

"Do you mind if they're all shorter?" asked Ellen.

"No. They could stand to have three inches off."

"Then I could do the same thing to all of them."

May smiled happily. "Could you really? That would be a nice Christmas present for me! And for Mum, too."

Mrs. Aitken agreed, and Ellen spent several evenings working at the curtains. When they were finished and rehung, no one would have known that John A. had put a hole in one of them.

Ellen was glad that she had been able to do something for Mrs. Aitken and May, but Hilda was the one she really wanted to give a present to and she had nothing for her. As she wound the left-over yarn neatly into a ball, she had an idea. She could make the extra cotton into a collar for Hilda, if Mrs. Aitken would give it to her.

"Yes, you may have it. I have a pattern book here some-where. There's a pretty collar in it."

The work went quickly and Ellen finished in plenty of time. Every day while they practised for the concert and talked about Christmas, Ellen smiled inwardly, thinking about her surprise.

While the children were decorating the school room on the afternoon of December 23rd, a snowstorm swooped down from the northwest. Hilda looked out anxiously two or three times and then about two o'clock decided to send the children home.

"What about our concert?" asked Dorothy.

"No concert I'm afraid," answered Hilda. "The storm looks like a bad one. No one will be able to get to school tomorrow. We'll have an extra day on our holiday and all come back after New Years Day."

Bradley punched Michael on the arm. "Hooray!" he shouted.

Miranda and Dorothy whimpered.

"Never mind, we'll have our concert another time," Hilda assured them, as she tied their scarves snugly. "Now, everyone go home as quickly as you can."

The storm continued all the next day until darkness fell. At the Aitkens' house preparations for Christmas dinner went ahead, even though no one knew whether the guests would be able to come.

When Mr. Aitken came in from the barn he reassured them. "It's a beautiful evening. Tomorrow will be fine. No trouble about travelling tomorrow."

"Good!" said May. "It would be awful to miss the concert and our Christmas party. Do you think Bill will come tonight to read his part?"

"No reason why not, as far as I can see," answered her father.

But Bill did not come. Ellen took his place in the Bible reading of the Christmas story that had become a tradition with the Aitken family on Christmas Eve. Next day, about mid-morning, while everyone was busy at tasks in preparation for the dinner, Bill stamped into the kitchen, calling "Merry Christmas!"

"Why didn't you come last night?" demanded his younger sister.

"Couldn't! Unexpectedly delayed!" he answered. He pulled her long braid and sang, "Ding! Dong! Christmas bells!"

"Don't Bill! You'll muss it! Why couldn't you come?"

"Because," answered Bill with a smile for Ellen, "I went into town yesterday and got back very late."

His mother turned to him with an anxious frown. "To town? In that storm? Whatever for?"

"Well," Bill answered, "I thought if Ellen's uncle had written a letter and it was in the Post Office in Patterson, it would be a shame not to have it for Christmas. So, I went to see."

Ellen stopped stirring the gravy. She felt goose bumps rising on her arms. She was afraid to breathe.

"Was there a letter?" asked May.

The young man, alarmed at Ellen's white face, pulled an envelope from his pocket. "Yes, there was," he said.

Ellen dropped the spoon with a clatter and would have swayed into the hot stove if Hilda had not pulled her onto a chair. She reached out a trembling hand and took the letter from Bill.

"Oh, Ellen," breathed Hilda, with a catch in her voice. "At last!"

Mr. Aitken blew his nose.

May flung her arms around Bill and hugged him. "What a great Christmas present!" she exclaimed.

Mrs. Aitken patted Ellen's arm. "Would you like to take your letter upstairs to read?" she asked very gently.

Ellen nodded. The woman wrapped a hot brick in a quilt that was heating behind the stove and handed it to her. Fred held open the stairway door and in a daze Ellen walked through the kitchen and up the stairs, hugging the bundle and staring at the letter.

In the bedroom she wrapped herself in the quilt and sat on the bed with the brick at her feet. For a few more moments she held the envelope in her hand, hardly daring to believe it was real. After all this time, Uncle Bert had finally written. She opened the letter and began to read.

Dear Little Nellie,

I was so happy to get your letter—two letters, in fact. It was like a voice from the grave. I was sure you were dead—drowned in the River Mersey. When you didn't come home that night, I went down to the dock looking for you. I asked questions of everyone I could see and heard about the fire and two kids running away. Someone said one of them was a flower girl. I knew you weren't a thief but I thought maybe something frightened you and you were hiding. Well when you didn't come back that night—and what a long miserable night it was—I went back next day to look for you. The policeman down there showed me the hat and basket they'd fished out of the river. People said they remembered seeing you on the edge of the quay and then you just disappeared. The copper said you must've drowned and he'd let me know when your body was found. At first I wouldn't believe him. I thought you were scared and hiding some-where and you'd come home or send me a message. But after a week, I had to believe it. I nearly went crazy.

You're all the family I have and I thought I'd lost you. I couldn't bear to stay around the city any longer so I got a job with a travelling troupe and went on a tour of the northern shires. I didn't tell anyone where I was going. Who would care? You were the only person who mattered. Then when the tour finished and the troupe broke up, I thought I'd go back to Liverpool. Just imagine my surprise when old Zeb, the doorman at the Lyceum Theatre, said he had a letter for me he'd been holding for weeks. As soon as I saw the writing, I knew it was from you! You could have knocked me over with a feather!

I pulled a box over to the door so as to get some light and sat and read it. I guess I must have turned pale, because old Zeb, he shuffled over with his bottle of spirits and told me to take a nip. 'Tis a good cure for bad news,' he says. 'Bad news!' says I. 'It's good news! The best in the world!' Well, I was sorry there was only old Zeb to share it with so off I went and looked up some of our old friends—Patty and the Priestleys and old Sal—do you remember? I told them all and were they glad!

Now, as to getting you home. It's going to take a lot of money. I've got two regular jobs and I pick up a little extra any way I can. Don't you fret. I'm saving every shilling and sometime, somehow, I'll have enough to pay for your passage home. Those seem like nice folks you're living with. I hope you can stay there until I send for you. Be a good girl and write to me soon.

With much love, dear Ellen, from your Uncle Bert.

For a long time, Ellen sat staring at the letter. Although she had never doubted that Uncle Bert loved her and wanted her back, as the weeks went by with no letter, she began to fear that something had happened to him. Maybe she would never see him again. Whenever that thought had come, she had pushed it to the back of her mind. Tears of relief now poured down her cheeks.

After some time, Hilda came into the room. She sat on the bed beside Ellen and hugged her tightly.

"Uncle Bert's going to send money for me to go home," Ellen said.

"Is he? When?"

Ellen sighed. "Not for a long time, maybe. It's a lot of money."

"Well," said Hilda, "I'm glad you'll be staying for a while longer. I'll miss you when you go." Gently she wiped the tears from Ellen's face.

Downstairs, Ellen showed the letter to everyone. They all shared her happiness.

The Christmas party was a joyous affair. Mr. Aitken's two big wild geese, stuffed with sage dressing, were the highlight of the dinner. For dessert, they had a huge steamed pudding filled with raisins and dried apples. The Ransome boys contributed a large fruit cake that had come in their Christmas parcel from home. Fred passed around a tin of English biscuits. But Priscilla gave them the biggest surprise. She had managed to save twelve fresh apples from the barrel she'd received from Ontario in October.

"How ever did you keep them?" asked her mother-in-law.

"It wasn't easy!" Sam answered. "Prissy fussed more about those apples than she did about the baby! They mustn't be too warm or they'd wrinkle. They mustn't be too cold or they'd freeze. They had to be hidden any time one of you came over. Eat them up so we can stop worrying about them!"

When the dishes were done, a few gifts were exchanged. Mrs. Aitken gave Ellen and May bright red toques and scarves. They were a complete surprise, as they had never seen her knitting anything but dark wool. Hilda was delighted with her collar. She pinned it on her blue dress immediately.

Ellen said shyly to Bill, "I wish I had a present for you to thank you for bringing me my letter."

"You already gave me a present," he said quietly.

"Did I? What?"

"The look on your face when you came downstairs."

"Come on Ellen," called May. "We need you! We're going to sing carols."

They sang carols and told stories of other Christmasses until it was time for the guests to go home and do chores.

On winter nights May and Ellen usually said their prayers under the warm covers, but that night Ellen knelt by the bed on the cold floor and gave thanks for the happiest day of her life. Then she went to sleep with Uncle Bert's letter under her pillow.

Chapter 8

It was a good thing Ellen had her letter to remind her there was a warmer place on earth than Manitoba. She couldn't believe the cold of those bright January days! Everything was frozen solid. Mr. Aitken or Fred drove the girls to school in the morning, but they walked home as usual, arriving just as the sun and the temperature sank again.

Ellen got itchy toes from sticking her cold feet as soon as she could get her mocassins off into the warm oven every day. They nearly drove her crazy.

"What a country!" said Fred one day, as he watched Ellen rub her sore feet. He had just spent half an hour thawing the pump to get a pail of water for the kitchen. He held his hands over the range and rubbed them together. "Don't you wish we were home?" he asked.

"Oh, yes!" agreed Ellen.

"What's it like in England now?" asked May.

"Warmer than here!" declared Fred. "Damp, though," he admitted.

Ellen remembered last January. She had spent the month indoors with a racking cough. For almost two weeks she'd been in bed. Uncle Bert had been scared. "Your mother died of consumption you know," he had said. "Don't you leave me Nellie." When she wrote again she must tell him that she hadn't coughed all winter.

"I don't know which is worse," she moaned, "itchy feet or a cough."

"A cough," replied Mrs. Aitken promptly. "Ellen, I keep telling you that you cause your own problems. How many times have I told you not to put your feet in the oven? Let them warm up gradually."

"But they're so cold! I can't walk."

"Cheer up child," Mr. Aitken said. "It won't last forever. You're not going to admit you can't take a little cold are you?"

But one morning, when he came in from the barn, he said, "No school today Charlotte. There's a storm brewing."

"A bad one?" she asked, as he lifted down a long coil of rope from a hook beside the door.

"Looks like it. It's snowing now."

May breathed on the frosted window and peeked out the little hole she made. "Is it windy?" she asked.

"Right. We're in for a blizzard."

"Oh," said Ellen, excited. "Am I going to see a blizzard?"

"You won't like it!" declared Mrs. Aitken.

Her husband went out with the rope.

"What's that for?" asked Ellen.

"He's going to rig a line from the house to the barn," explained May. "If it's a real blizzard, you won't be able to see more than a few inches in front of your face. He'll use the rope to guide him when he goes to tend the animals."

Ellen shivered with fear. Then she stood at May's peep-hole and watched the snow pile up in tiny drifts on the window sill. Almost mesmerized by the dancing flakes, she jumped when a gust of wind battered the pane with hard pellets.

The storm increased in fury as the hours passed. By mid-afternoon the farmhouse was totally isolated. Inside, the kitchen formed a fortress inside the cold-gripped house, the area around the stove, the only spot really comfortable. The circle of warmth was very small in spite of the roaring fire. Every time he added wood, Mr. Aitken looked anxiously at the red-hot stovepipes. Two lanterns, one hanging from the ceiling and one on the table, occasionally flickered as drafts blew in. An extra inch of frost had been added to the windows. Frost had even formed on the door to Fred's room.

Ellen winced when a particularly loud crack came from upstairs.

"Just the wall creaking in the cold," said Mrs. Aitken. "Go on May."

May was reading *David Copperfield* aloud while the others worked: Mrs. Aitken knitting a sock, Ellen hemming a sheet and Mr. Aitken mending a harness. Sometimes she almost had to shout to be heard above the shrieking of the wind. When she came to the end of the chapter she closed the book. No one objected. Mrs. Aitken was mentally counting her family members. Fred was working with Sam for a few days. Sam would know enough to stay close to home this morning and so would Bill. Even if Hilda had gone to school early, the storm gave plenty of warning to those who could read the signs and she'd be safe back at the Meadow farm in good time. Wilf, May and Ellen were all here, safe and sound. She hoped no poor soul was out in the storm.

Mr. Aitken was wondering whether he would be able to get out to the barn in the morning. Even though he knew the animals were safe and had plenty of food, he didn't like to go a whole day without looking at them. Thank goodness there had been time to rig up a 'lifeline' from the barn to the house. He had known farmers to lose their way in their own yards during a blizzard and freeze to death when they couldn't find the house again.

At first Ellen had been fascinated by the swirling snow and howling wind. For a while it was fun to be shut up in the cozy house with no chores to do and no school to attend. But the storm went on and on. They were all safe and warm, but what if someone was out in the storm. How long could a person live out there?

May was thinking of having to go to bed in the freezing room upstairs. Mrs. Aitken was so fussy about everything being proper. She didn't even like her husband taking a nap in the rocking chair in the kitchen—bedrooms were the proper place for sleeping. Why couldn't they all sleep around the fire tonight? She picked up her knitting instead of the book.

Ellen listened to the wind. It sounded like a hundred people all screaming together. She shuddered. Then she put down her sewing and listened intently. Was someone calling? No, it was just the wind. Wait! There it was again. She looked at the others, all absorbed in their work.

"Did you hear anything?" she asked.

"Hear what?" asked Mrs. Aitken. "The wind? The house creaking?"

"I don't know. A sound. Something bumping. Someone calling."

Mr. Aitken said, "It's just the wind. Sometimes it does sound like shouting or screaming. You'll get used to it. You'll really enjoy the sound of silence when this is over."

Ellen picked up the sheet, took two stitches and put it down again. She got up and walked toward the window. The air was icy. She hugged herself.

"Come back to the fire Ellen," said May. "You'll freeze over there."

Then Ellen heard it quite clearly. A human voice calling. Or moaning.

She turned anxiously to the others. "Listen! Don't you hear it?"

Mr. Aitken walked over to Ellen and turned his ear to the wall.

"It's just the wind Ellen," he said. "Come and sit down."

Ellen obeyed. They had all been through blizzards before. They must be right.

But in two minutes, she jumped up again.

"There *is* someone out there!" she exclaimed. "There is! Listen!"

An extra hard gust rattled the windows.

"You're just imagining things Ellen," Mrs. Aitken said. "Help me fix the vegetables for supper. It will take your mind off the storm. Luckily, we have plenty up here so no one has to go down to the cellar."

"Please Mrs. Aitken! I can hear someone! Let me go and see. Please!"

"No," shouted May. "You'd get lost right away! Don't you know that? As soon as you stepped out the door you'd be lost. Dad! Mum! Don't let her go!"

"Of course you can't go out Ellen. You don't understand. No one could live out there now."

"But there is someone out there," Ellen said tearfully.

Once again they all listened intently.

"I don't hear anything. Do you Wilf?"

"Only the wind," answered her husband. He watched Ellen pace back and forth from the window to the door. She looked so wretched that he finally said, "I'll go and see."

"No Dad," whimpered May.

"Wilf, do you really think you should?" asked his wife.

"I won't let go of the rope. If I can't see or hear anything, I'll come right back."

It took a long time for him to dress. At last his wife thought that he was properly equipped.

She and May stood by to close the door after him, but before they could do so against the brutal force of the wind, a mound of snow had blown in.

Ellen felt terribly guilty as she watched his mittened hand grope for the thick, ice-coated rope.

Waiting was agony. Mrs. Aitken moved the lantern from the table to the windowsill, and then went on peeling potatoes. Her rigid back and tilted head indicated that she was straining to hear. May asked sarcastically every few minutes, "Can you hear anything Ellen?"

Ellen shook her head miserably. Now she could hear only

---

the wind. But she had heard something else before. She had!

After what seemed like an hour there was a great thump at the door. Ellen flew to open it. May and her mother were right behind her. Two snow-covered bundles stood there. One thrust the other inside, saying in Mr. Aitken's voice, "Take care of him. I'm going to put his horse in the barn." Then he was gone and his wife caught the other form in her arms and lugged it to a chair.

"Blankets! Quickly May," she ordered.

May raced upstairs with no thought of the cold.

"Fetch the broom Ellen. Brush the snow off. Gently, girl! Gently! Now help me take off his things."

I was right! I was right! thought Ellen. I did hear someone! Oh, the poor man! Her insides knotted and she shrank back a little when she caught sight of the white skin and dull eyes as they unwound a long, icy scarf from the man's bearded face.

May returned with an armful of blankets. She hung two from the towel rack above the stove and wrapped two more around bricks that were being heated to warm their beds.

"Who is it Mum?" she asked quietly.

"I don't know. A stranger."

She stripped off his double mittens and began chaffing one hand. Ellen rubbed the other. She had never felt anything so cold and lifeless. Her fear showed in her eyes as she looked appealingly at Mrs. Aitken. The woman shook her head slightly.

"Can you pull him forward Ellen? she asked. "I want to take his coat off."

The man groaned as his stiff body tilted on to Ellen's

chest. Snow seeped through her dress. May helped her mother and they finally wrestled him out of his coat. May draped a warm blanket over the back of the chair. Mrs. Aitken tilted the man against it and wrapped it closely around him. A spark of life returned to his eyes. He seemed to be trying to smile, but his lips were too stiff.

Mrs. Aitken had been watching his face anxiously. Now she turned to Ellen and smiled. "Don't look so worried. He's going to be fine." Ellen gasped. "If you hadn't heard him..." Mrs. Aitken said with a shake of her head. Suddenly, she became brisk again. "Now for his boots. His feet may be frozen."

They couldn't undo the icy laces. When Mr. Aitken came in, he said the boots would have to thaw a little before they could remove them. In the meantime May had made tea. Her mother held a steaming cup to the man's lips. His fingers were too numb for him to hold the cup himself, but he managed to sip a few mouthfuls. The two girls were told to make supper while the adults undressed their visitor and wrapped him in blankets. At first, frightened by what had nearly happened and embarrassed by what was going on behind them, the girls worked in silence.

May kept glancing at Ellen and finally she whispered. "You saved his life you know. Another few minutes and he'd have been dead. How did you know he was there?"

"I heard him call. I told you."

"I didn't hear him. Neither did Mum or Dad. How did you?"

"I can't tell. I just knew someone was there," Ellen answered.

Mr. Aitken, too, praised Ellen's hearing as they all sat

around the table and relived the event. The man they had saved only stopped saying thanks long enough to eat the hot food and only stopped eating long enough to say thanks. He spoke English poorly, but they understood him.

He told them he was German and farmed in the Dauphin district, many miles to the north. When the blizzard struck very suddenly, he was cutting wood in the forest a few miles south of his home. Knowing that his wife would be anxious about him, he started for home with half a load of logs. After a very short while, he was completely lost and could only trust the horse to lead him home. He knew that he must keep moving. Once, the load partly upset and he managed to right the sled. The next time it happened, the sled turned completely over so he cut the traces and freed the horse. He was so stiff from the cold that he couldn't mount the animal. He trudged by its side for mile after mile in the wrong direction. He must have passed fairly close to other houses, but he saw none through the snow until the horse bumped into the corner of the Aitken's front porch. Even then, he was sure he would die because he had no strength to crawl further or to shout above the wind. When Mr. Aitken bent over him, he couldn't believe that his rescuer was real.

"What a blessing to me, your little girl's ears," he said.

As he left the next day, he said, "I wish I was not such a poor man. I have nothing to give the girl who saved my life."

Ellen and the Aitkens all exclaimed together. "No! No! We're just thankful she heard you."

"I will think of something," he called back as his horse picked its way through the snowdrifts.

Chapter 9

One day, just before supper, Ellen was carrying a pail of water back to the house when she heard sleigh bells. For the first time since November, she was not wearing mittens. The family had warned her that this was just a short February thaw and cold weather would soon return to stay for another two months. Ellen was not sure whether to believe this. For her, the winter had been far too long already. The soft snow and almost-warm breeze seemed a promise of spring, just as the sleigh bells coming nearer promised visitors. Maybe it was a neighbour who had been to town and was bringing mail, perhaps a letter from Uncle Bert.

She hurried inside. As she passed Mr. Aitken having his pre-supper doze in the rocking chair, she said, "Someone coming!"

He sat up slowly and rubbed his hands over his face and bald head. Fred put down his newspaper and went out to look after the horse.

When the cutter came into view through the kitchen window, Mrs. Aitken said, "Why it's Mrs. Logan from the Orphan Society. Let's look at you, child. Are you tidy?" She pulled Ellen's collar straight and pushed some wisps of hair off her forehead. "I wish there was time to rebraid your hair."

Mr. Aitken winked at Ellen. "Don't fuss Charlotte," he said. "She looks fine."

Mrs. Logan was accompanied by a boy who stopped just inside the door. He took one swift, fearful glance around the room. Catching sight of Ellen, his eyes brightened briefly, then a sullen mask returned to cover his dirty face. He stood with his knees slightly flexed as though ready to run and with one shoulder hunched and his arm ready to fly up as if to ward off a blow. Ellen stared at him. Was that George?

"How are you?" Mrs. Aitken asked the visitor.

"I'm angry!" answered Mrs. Logan. "Look at this."

Gently, she pulled the boy toward her and removed his hat. Pushing aside the matted hair, she revealed a large ugly bruise running from his temple to his ear.

Yes, it was George! Ellen recognized his protruding ears! But one ear was now red and so swollen that it did not stick out much. Ellen cringed and she heard Mrs. Aitken gasp.

"Who did it?" asked Mr. Aitken. The cold anger in his voice made Ellen's scalp prickle with fear.

"Alf Black," answered the supervisor.

"He should be horsewhipped!" Neither May nor Ellen had ever heard that harsh tone before.

"He should!" agreed Mrs. Logan. "Look here!" She

stripped off George's overcoat and pulled up the sleeves of the ill-fitting shirt he wore. His bony wrists and hands were chapped and red, the knuckles swollen and cracked. "Black's evidently starved the boy. He's beaten him, kept him from school, abused him in every way. Naturally I took the boy from him. I knew you'd give him a bed for tonight."

"Of course! Of course!" Mrs. Aitken said. "Poor child! Come and sit down," she urged the boy, but he didn't move.

"He won't talk," warned Mrs. Logan. "I haven't been able to get a word out of him."

George not talk! Ellen looked at him carefully. His face was grey with deep, dark circles under the eyes. Ragged, dirty clothes hung on his pitifully thin body. He seemed to have no spirit left. As she gazed at him in horror, Ellen began to tremble. She was remembering the time on the ship when she had said, "I hope he goes to the meanest family in Canada!" But she hadn't meant it! She hadn't wanted this to happen!

Mrs. Aitken decided George would have to bathe before the family sat down with him to supper. Her husband carried the tin tub into Fred's room and Fred filled it with warm water meant for the dishes. Ellen had to refill the pail. Fred came back to report bruises and welts all over George's body.

"That was Black's way of teaching, apparently! If the kid didn't know how to do something, the oaf beat him till he learned. Poor kid! Why was he ever sent to such a man?"

In a defensive tone the Orphan Society representative replied, "When Alf Black applied for an orphan, his wife was still living. He never told the Society about his wife's death.

I suppose he needed farm help more than ever then, and just decided to take the boy. When I saw him in October, there was a housekeeper there, or so I was told."

George came out of Fred's bedroom just then wearing clean clothes belonging to the hired man. Ellen had to cover her mouth to hide a giggle. Fred was not a big man, but his pants and shirt hung on George like clothes on a scarecrow. When she caught sight of his eyes, Ellen sobered. This boy wasn't the George she knew!

Mrs. Logan asked him, "How long did the woman stay?"

"She went away with the threshing gang," he answered.

"And who cooked then?" Mrs. Aitken asked. "Did you?"

"No Ma'am. Mr. Black cooked mostly. 'Cept when he came back from town drunk. Then he didn't want to eat, just drink—so I got my own."

"I might have known!" said Mrs. Aitken, tight-lipped. "The demon rum! Well come along all. Sit down to supper now."

George watched his plate being heaped with fluffy biscuits and beef stew full of big chunks of carrots, turnips and potatoes as well as meat and thick gravy. After taking two small, polite forkfuls, he seemed to forget everyone around him as he absorbed that plateful and another almost as big. Ellen and May stared as he devoured a second piece of apple pie. Sometimes at home in England, Ellen and Uncle Bert had gone without a meal when they were low on money, but she had never seen anyone as famished as George appeared to be.

Mr. Aitken reached over and pulled at the floppy shirt sleeve. "I can actually see these clothes filling out, " he said with a twinkle in his eye. George looked at him with such a scared face that he hastily added, "Now then son! I was only teasing! You're welcome to all you can eat. Charlotte, another piece of pie for the boy."

"Not now Wilf. You'll only make him sick with more. Don't look so worried George. No one here begrudges you food."

While the girls were doing the dishes and the two men were out in the barn, the ladies sat at the table taking tucks in some of Bill's old clothes. George was kept at hand to try them on.

May asked him, "Why didn't you tell someone that man was starving you?"

"I never saw no one to tell."

"You never saw anyone all winter?" she echoed in astonishment.

"Not after the threshing gang left."

Mrs. Logan said, "It's a very isolated farm. There are no near neighbours. And Black never took him to town, it seems."

"You should have run away!" May declared. "I would have!"

"Where to?" asked George with a show of his old spirit.

"Exactly! Don't talk foolishly May," said her mother. "He would have been worse off lost in the bush in winter."

"I was going to run off in the spring," George muttered.

Ellen thought of the great empty spaces she and George had seen from the train back in August. She remembered how frightening the land looked. "It's a good thing Mrs. Logan came to check on you," she said with a shiver. "What did the old meanie say when he saw her?"

"Said he'd give me the worst thrashing of my life if I opened my yap."

"He didn't need to say a word, poor lamb!" Mrs. Logan said. "One look at him was enough. And the state of the house! Filthy! I'd only been at the place half an hour when I told Mr. Black to harness my horse. 'I'm taking the child from you, Mr. Black,' I said. 'And don't try to stop me! You'll be lucky if you're not prosecuted!' I said. He tried sweet talk and he tried threats, but he saw I meant what I said and he let us go."

Mr. Aitken came back in as she spoke. "What will you do with the boy now?" he asked.

Mrs. Logan sighed. "I don't know. I wish the Barnardo Farm at Russell was ready. I could have left him there until we found a new place. I suppose I'll send him to an orphanage in Winnipeg and ask them to keep him. There's a train from Patterson the day after tomorrow. May we stay here an extra night?"

"Of course! And very welcome!" the Aitkens said together.

When they were in bed, Ellen asked May whether there were many farmers like Alf Black.

"I hope not!" answered May. "What a terrible brute! Anyway don't worry yet. Did you see the way Mum and Dad looked at each other? I guess they've thought of a plan."

Next day after school they found out what that plan was.

"Where's Mrs. Logan and that George?" asked May when they came into the kitchen.

"Mrs. Logan has gone and George is over at Sam's," answered her mother. "He's going to live there."

"Lucky boy!" exclaimed May. "He'll get to play with Teddy every day!"

"He hasn't gone to play. He's gone to be their chore boy

as he was at Black's. But he'll be much better treated."

Ellen was glad George would not be mistreated, but she wasn't sure she wanted him to share in her family. But they're not my family, she thought, a little surprised at herself.

George did not go to school for another week. By that time the swelling on his ear had gone down and the dark circles under his eyes had faded. He was still wary and nervous though. On Monday morning, as he walked with May and Ellen, a prairie chicken whirred out of a snow-capped straw stack. He flinched and flung up his arm.

It took Ellen a long time to stop being suspicious of George's meekness. One day, when May had stayed behind to help Hilda, they were walking home by themselves after dropping Miranda at her corner. It was the first time they had been alone since George arrived.

"Do you like it at Sam and Prissy's?" Ellen asked him.

"No! I hate it! Oh, not them. They're not bad. It's the farm! Living in the country! I hate it!" He kicked at a blob of snow in the road. "Don't you? You're always talking about going home. Back to England."

"But I don't hate the country," said Ellen slowly. She gazed out over the white land. "Most of the time I like it here. It was sure pretty when I came in the summer and the snow's kind of nice."

"But farmers work so hard!"

"Yes. I don't mind when everyone is helping. It was bad for you when that Mr. Black made you do all the chores."

"He never! He worked hard too. Work never ends here. And it's so lonely! I like people around."

"You mean you want to go back to England?"

"No! I ain't ever going back! I'll stick it out till I'm sixteen and get my wages, then I'm heading for a city."

"What wages?"

"The money that's being saved for us. All us orphans get ten dollars a year until we're sixteen. Course you don't get it since you're not an orphan, so you say."

Ellen skipped for a few steps. "Maybe I do! Maybe I do have some money to go home!"

"Dummy! You can't get it for five more years."

After a glum silence, Ellen said, "It's funny. You hate this place, but you want to stay and I like it, but I want to leave."

"Well why do you want to go back?" George was beginning to sound like his old belligerent self.

"Because my uncle's there and he's my family."

"Maybe he don't want you!" said George nastily.

Ellen grabbed a handful of snow, but by the time she had shaped it into a ball George was far ahead.

The next weekend when Hilda was home, she said, "I've been thinking about our school concert, the one we didn't have at Christmas. Let's have it next Friday."

"Good idea," said her father. "It's been a long, hard winter. Everyone will be glad of a bit of fun."

Word spread around the district and everybody came, even the Winsteads, recently arrived from England. By ten o'clock on Friday morning, the school house was ringed with sleighs. As soon as they arrived, Lawrence's big brothers divided the children and young people into two teams and organized the building of the snow forts for a battle. Ellen helped Helen and Dorothy to roll big snowballs into a line to form the base of the wall. Then they chinked the spaces between the balls. Soon, their mittens and the knees of their stockings were caked with ice granules. George and Bradley threw more snow at the girls than they did at the fort until the walls of the rival fortress began to grow fast. Then they settled down to serious work. When the walls were too high for the younger children to reach, they were told to make a stockpile of snowballs for ammunition. Rudy Ferguson, who had come over from the next district, helped Hilda to make a slide from the tail board of his wagon. They piled bales of hay in a slope and covered them with snow. Mrs. Meadows supplied two tin trays and soon the youngest children were taking turns.

After a few minutes, Hilda called to Ellen. "Will you come and help Rudy? I have to go in now."

Ellen caught three more children at the bottom of the slope before a great shout went up from the forts. "We're ready for the war!"

"Your team's bigger than ours," said Phil Osborne. "Let us have Rudy."

"Fair enough!"

"I'd like that," called Rudy, "but I have a job here."

"I could do that job," said Mr. Winstead. "I'm not dressed for snowballing."

Wearing overshoes, a velvet-collared overcoat, leather gloves and a bowler hat, he was standing on the porch steps watching all the fun.

"And I'll help him," said Mrs. Meadows, who had just come out of the building. "You run and join the battle Ellen."

"I'll hit you first Rudy!" yelled Ellen, as she dashed to her fort.

The idea was to capture the other team's flag and get home with it without being snowballed. The battle raged back and forth with many falls on the slippery snow and much laughter.

In the midst of three cheers for the losers, Hilda came out and rang the brass hand bell. "Lunch time!"

Piles of sandwiches disappeared like melting snow as the hungry warriors attacked them. There was hot tea for the adults and cocoa for the children. Then came the cakes. Michael and Bradley made sure of two pieces each before the concert began. Later, they recited their poem with only a little prompting from Hilda. Mistakes or not, every effort was loudly applauded. Ellen sang two songs, both serious, as Mrs. Aitken did not approve of a young girl singing comic songs in public.

After everyone else had gone home, Sam and Bill and Rudy Ferguson cleared the room for Monday morning.

The sun was low in the sky when the big farm wagon, fitted with sleigh runners, carried the Aitken family homeward. Mr. Aitken drove the horse. Beside him on the box, well wrapped in furs, sat his wife and Prissy holding the baby. In the hay-filled wagon May, Hilda and Ellen snuggled together under one blanket. Fred and George had dug themselves nests in the hay, but Sam and Bill sat with their legs dangling over the open tailboard. The air was filled with the sounds of the squeaking runners on the snow, the clip-clop of the horses' hooves and the tinkling of the harness bells. Ellen leaned her head on Hilda's shoulder.

"Too much excitement?" Hilda asked.

"Oh, no! It was wonderful!"

Ellen wriggled with happiness. If only Uncle Bert was here life would be perfect.

When they were nearly home, Bill said, "Well big sister, I've been expecting you to make an announcement any minute."

Prissy turned around, laughing. "Me, too!"

Hilda's rosy cheeks turned even redder.

What were they talking about? wondered Ellen.

Sam said, "Out with it, Sis. We've all guessed."

"Don't be rude, Sam," scolded his mother. Turning to Hilda, she said, "You tell us when you're ready. Don't let the boys rush you."

Hilda blushed again. "Well, your guesses are right! Rudy Ferguson and I are going to be married."

It wasn't until they were alone that May noticed Ellen's white face and stricken eyes.

"Aren't you excited about the wedding?" asked May.

"Oh yes! It's lovely."

"You should be happy for Hilda. After all, they met because of you."

"Yes I am. It's just that she's going away and I won't see her again."

"Silly! Of course you will. She won't be married till the summer and she's not going far. Anyway, you'll be going back to England. Maybe you won't even be here for the wedding."

"Maybe not," answered Ellen. "Uncle Bert said he might have enough money by summer."

It was so long to wait. She wanted her uncle right now. Surely, when winter was over, she would hear good news from him.

Chapter 10

Winter did end and spring came at last. One April day, a V-shaped flock of Canada geese flew over heading north. Ellen and May saw it on their way home from school. The next day, Hilda wrote on the blackboard the rules for the first crow contest.

1. *You must see the bird, not just hear it.*
2. *There must be at least one witness.*

Just before noon one day, while the children were all busy at their desks, they were startled by a loud call from the other side of the blank wall. "Caw! Caw! Caw!" Without waiting for permission, Michael charged out the door and spotted the black bird high up on the bare branch of a poplar tree at the edge of the bush. The rest of the children, pouring out behind him, looked where he pointed, laughed and pounded one another for joy. Soon other birds would follow, the earth would thaw and life would return to the plants.

Shortly after that, school closed for a month. The snow

thawed rapidly, turning the earth into thick black goo. Neither horses nor humans could wade through it. Each farm was as isolated as it had been in the blizzard until the steady spring winds dried the earth. A carpet of blue prairie crocuses then covered the fields. In a few days the farmers began to seed and the boys were needed at home to help with the work. Suddenly one morning a great symphony broke out from the ponds and wet places as hundreds of frogs croaked. As Ellen listened in wonder, such a wave of homesickness washed through her that she felt physically ill.

Fred knew what was wrong with her. "I get it every spring," he said. "Homesickness. The first year I thought I'd die of it, but it's not so bad now."

Mrs. Aitken also understood and sympathized. She had felt twinges of longing for her home in Ontario. Still, just in case there was a physical cause for the illness, she dosed both Ellen and May with sulphur and molasses.

"Ugh!" said May, shivering violently and twisting her face into a horrible grimace. "That's the very last time I'm ever going to swallow that stuff! Next year, I'll be fourteen and I won't, won't, *won't* take it."

Ellen was so astonished at the evil taste of the medicine that she couldn't speak at all. Nor did the dose cure the homesickness. For several days she suffered from loss of appetite, tummy pains and headache. Her mood swung from longing to be with Uncle Bert to hating him for not yet sending the money for her to go home.

"The best cure for spring fever," said Hilda, "is a new dress and a different hairstyle. Let me cut your hair."

Before, whenever anyone suggested that her hair would

be easier to manage if it were shorter, Ellen had refused to cut it. She didn't want to look different when her uncle saw her again. But she knew that she did look different. She was about two inches taller and no longer painfully skinny. She allowed Hilda to cut off the heavy braid. Washed with tar soap in rain water, her hair, shiny and chestnut colored, hung to her shoulders in soft waves. Everyone except May admired it. Ellen decided May was jealous because her hair was straight as a poker and could not be curled.

One Saturday morning after they had been back to school for a week, Ellen was making butter in the milk house. Her arm ached from cranking the heavy handle of the churn. Her back had a crick in it from standing so long in one position. She had just lifted the lid of the churn for the sixth time and heaved a sigh of relief at the first tiny lump of yellow, when she heard May call to her.

"Ellen! Come here! Someone to see you!" There was laughter in May's voice.

Who could it be? She hesitated. Mrs. Aitken might be angry if she left the butter making now.

May appeared in the doorway. "Come on Ellen," she said impatiently. "Mum said you were to come."

Ellen followed her. May giggled and nodded to a group of people standing in the lane beside a wagon pulled by an old, tired-looking horse. There was a bearded man dressed in overalls and a black suit coat, with a wide-brimmed felt hat in his hands. Ellen recognized him at once.

Beside him stood his wife, holding a baby. She wore a long, black skirt, a black shawl and a blue kerchief on her head. Two children had shyly tucked themselves behind their mother's skirt. A third child, the tallest, stood in front of the father with a covered reed basket held carefully in his hands.

Mrs. Aitken called, "Come here Ellen. Mr. Freisen wants to give you something."

"Yah! A little present for saving my life. My wife and my children..." he pointed to each of them "... were all glad to see me home again that bad day. I tell them about the little girl with the so sharp ears."

"Come and see what it is Ellen. They won't come in for a cup of tea until you do."

The boy held out the basket and Ellen reached to take it from him. But he didn't let go. Tucking it under one arm, he unfastened the peg at the side. The lid popped up and a little black and white kitten poked its head out and tried to scramble out of the basket. Ellen laughed aloud and caught the tiny creature in both hands. It escaped and ran up her arm, across her back and perched on the other shoulder. It sniffed her cheek, pawed at her hair and started down her arm. Then it changed its mind, came back and settled snugly into the hollow at the base of her neck. Ellen felt the soft fur against her cheek and listened to the tiny purr.

Looking at Mrs. Aitken, she asked, "Is it really mine?"

Mrs. Aitken nodded. "Yes. It seems to think so."

The guests stayed just long enough to drink tea and lemonade. Only the father spoke English, so conversation was difficult and they had a long drive home. Mrs. Aitken told Ellen how precious the gift was. In rural Manitoba there were very few cats. How could she thank the Freisen family? She had nothing of her own except some hair ribbons. If she were in England, she would make up a bouquet. Well, why not? There was Queen Anne's Lace and buttercups growing around the vegetable patch. And foxtail grass near the front steps. By the time the wagon was loaded, she had made a pretty arrangement tied with her best red ribbon. She handed it to Mrs. Freisen with a wide smile. Then she took the kitten from May and held it aloft until they were out of sight.

Later, when Ellen came in after finishing the churning, May was playing with the kitten on the kitchen floor.

"Look at the white mark on her chest Ellen," she said. "You'll have to call her Star."

Ellen grabbed the kitten and hugged it fiercely. "No!" she said. "Her name is... is... Sky."

"I was only playing with it," said May, pouting.

Mr. Aitken was delighted with Ellen's cat. "By harvest time she'll be a good mouser. No more holes nibbled in the grain sacks."

Ellen was allowed to keep the kitten in the kitchen for a few days, but after that it had to go out in the barn. Once she had taught him that she wouldn't be herded like the cows or frightened like the chickens, Sky got on very well with John A.

For a few days the girls at school talked only about Ellen's kitten. Then one day Florrie Osborne said proudly, "We had our picture taken on Saturday. A man named Mr. O'Reilly took it with a camera. We all dressed up and Mum and Dad sat on the porch and us kids stood beside them. We're going to send it to our grandparents in Ontario."

CHARLES O'REILLY, PORTRAIT TAKER AND PHOTOGRAPHER OF THE SCENIC BEAUTY OF THE NORTH-WEST, toured around the Onala District in a small, horse-drawn wagon with a large box built on the back. It held his equipment and samples of his work. He found plenty of customers during the warm, bright days of that April. One Saturday, he arrived at the Aitken farm in time to eat the noon meal with them.

"They say he has the gift of the gab," Mr. Aitken had warned the family earlier. "We'll tell him what we want before he gets into his sales pitch."

"Right then," agreed Mr. O'Reilly cheerfully. "One picture of the house with the six of you on the porch. And a second pose with the four Aitkens—not so much of the building, I guess? Right! What about you Mr. Harder? Will you surprise the folks at home with a portrait? They'll have forgotten how good-looking you are."

Fred said, "No one wants my picture! I was thinking, though, I'd pay for Ellen to have one done, if I could afford it. Her uncle might not recognize her unless he sees how much she's changed."

"What a good idea Fred!" cried Hilda. "I'll pay half, shall I?"

"Oh, thank you! Thank you both!" Ellen said.

When Ellen was tidied up, she went outside and joined Fred and the photographer who were standing at the open double doors at the back of the van. She heard the clink of crockery and caught a whiff of something she hadn't smelled since coming to the farm—alcohol.

"Here comes the family," said Mr. O'Reilly. He slammed the door quickly.

He handed Fred a wooden box full of large square photographic plates and then picked up the big camera set on tripod legs.

It took a long time to arrange everyone to Mr. O'Reilly's

satisfaction. Five times he ducked under the black cloth at the back of the camera and ordered them to move one way or another.

At last he said, "Now that's it. That will be a grand photograph. You must all keep perfectly still until I say you can move." He held up a stick with some brightly colored feathers on it. "This is my birdie," he said. "I want you all to keep your eyes on the birdie until I take it down. Not too stiff please Mr. Aitken. Fine. Ready now. Everybody look at the birdie. Don't move a muscle."

Long before the time was up, the feathers of the birdie had blurred in Ellen's vision, but she didn't dare to blink.

"My nose was so itchy," exclaimed May, as soon as the photographer released them.

He laughed as he transferred the heavy plate from the camera to the box and replaced it with another. "Give it a good rub before this one," he suggested. "I'll come in a little closer for the four of you."

While he arranged the Aitkens, Ellen ran to find Sky.

Mr. Reilly frowned. "Animals can't keep still," he said.

Ellen promised she would hold her tight, but after thirty seconds she knew she had made a mistake. When the photographer returned with the pictures the next week, Ellen's portrait was very life-like, but the blur in her arms could have been anything.

"Never mind," said Hilda. "It's you we want your uncle to see."

Within a week, Bill had to go to town. He took the photograph and mailed it to England. For days Ellen daydreamed about how Uncle Bert would feel when he received it.

Chapter 11

A week after the picture started on its way, May brought home an invitation from the Johnson family. Steve Johnson and his bride were building a new house. The outside walls were up and the roof on, but before partitioning the inside into rooms they planned to have a dance for the whole district.

"There'll be liquor I suppose," said Mrs. Aitken.

"Bound to be at the Johnson's place," answered her husband. "Still, I think we must go. Wouldn't be neighbourly not to."

"Yes I suppose you and I must go, but I don't want May and Ellen there. It'll be no place for little girls if I know anything of young men and liquor."

"Only thing is," said Mr. Aitken, "what about that sow? She still needs attention. Fred and I can't both be away for hours."

Not long ago, the pigs had broken down their sty fence by leaning their combined weight on it. Before they were recaptured, one sow had gashed her right hind leg. For a time she wouldn't let Fred near it. The sore became infected. He had been applying fresh poultices every two hours.

"I'll stay home," said Fred. "You and your wife should both go."

"Can you manage that pig alone?" asked his boss.

"Yes. To be honest, she's more restless with you around."

May and Ellen felt better about missing the dance when Prissy left the baby with them. "He'll sleep much better in this quiet house," she said.

The girls played with Teddy for a couple of hours, then May fed him his supper and rocked him to sleep while Ellen prepared a meal. When it was ready, she struck the triangle outside the back door to call Fred in from the barn. It was a pleasant evening so Ellen left the back door open. From her place at the table May could see out to the barn.

"What's Fred doing?" she asked with a little frown.

Ellen turned to look out the window. The hired man, stepping carefully and deliberately, was tacking across the farm yard as though he were a sailboat coming up the harbour. There was a foolish smile on his face and he was singing quietly to himself.

Ellen grinned. "Looks like he's drunk," she said.

"Drunk!" exclaimed May, scandalized and frightened.

She got up and went to the door. Fred was on the bottom step. With the door half-closed she demanded, "What's wrong with you?"

"Wrong? Wrong with me? There's nothing wrong with me." Fred's words were slurred.

Ellen peeked over May's arm. "You've been drinking haven't you?" she asked.

For a moment Fred looked indignant, then he smirked. "Well, just a little," he said. "I just had a tiny drop. Can't go to the party. Have my own party."

"Where did you get it?" asked May angrily.

Fred wagged a finger at her. "Oh no, that's my secret. I'm not telling."

"It was Mr. O'Reilly, wasn't it?" Ellen asked.

"Yes," admitted Fred. "Brought me a bottle when he came back with the pictures. Good stuff."

He moved up one step. May closed the door further.

"You can't come in here," she said through the crack.

"What about my supper?" said Fred in a tearful voice.

Seeing that May was really frightened, Ellen said, "I'll put his supper on a plate and he can take it to the barn."

"Right-oh," said Fred cheerfully.

When he had gone, May closed the door with a bang. "What are we going to do? Mum and Dad won't be back for hours."

"Fred isn't going to hurt us," answered Ellen. "Don't worry! He'll fall asleep after a while and in the morning he'll have a headache."

"How do you know so much about it?" demanded May.

"Uncle Bert used to take a drop too much sometimes." At May's shocked expression, she added, "Men do, you know."

"Not the men I know!"

Ellen shrugged. She thought May was taking the whole thing much too seriously. What harm could come of it?

The two girls ate almost in silence. May refused to let Ellen go to the barn to get Fred's plate, but after their own dishes were washed she let her take the dishpan outside to pour the water on the garden. She stood on the stoop with the doorknob in her hand, ready to leap inside and slam the door if necessary.

"Any sign of him?" she called softly, as Ellen started back.

"No," answered Ellen. She stood looking toward the barn. All was quiet there. One big door was slightly ajar, but not far enough for Ellen to see inside in the failing light. Then a tiny thread of smoke wafted through the opening.

The dishpan fell from Ellen's hand. "May! Look!"

May leaped down the stairs.

"Fire!" she said.

She raced toward the barn, Ellen at her heels. Just inside the door, in a nest of hay, Fred lay sleeping. John A. crouched nearby sniffing and whining at a smouldering hay bale. On top of the bale, Fred's pipe hung upside down over the edge of his supper plate.

"Fred! Fred! Wake up!" yelled May. He only snored louder. "It's useless! He's dead to the world!"

She grabbed the fire bucket near the door and threw the water on the bale. "Get another bucket," she ordered Ellen, as she raced to the pump to refill hers.

Ellen flew into the house and out again to take May's place at the pump while she ran back to the fire with her half bucket of water.

They each made another frantic trip as Fred slept peacefully on.

Flames broke out of the dry end of the bale and spread to some loose straw. The cattle were beginning to bawl from fear and still Fred slept.

Ellen threw her next bucket of water over him.

Sputtering, he sat up and looked around groggily.

"Wake up Fred!" Ellen shouted. "Fire! Help us!"

All color left Fred's face. He scrambled to his feet and raced out to the pump. His strong arm filled both buckets in a quarter of the time it had taken the girls. They each carried three more pailfuls to the barn and then the fire was out.

Fred took the bale outside and broke it open. Back inside, he spread the straw around and checked the floor and stall post for embers. No trace of the fire remained.

May glared at the hired man. Like all farmers, she was terrified of fire which could wipe out years of work in hours. She had been badly frightened. Her shoes, stockings and skirt were soaked with water. Her upper arm ached where the pump handle had caught it as she fled with her first pailful.

"You're not allowed to smoke in the barn!" she said accusingly. "Just wait till Dad gets home and sees this mess."

Fred prodded some of the wet straw into a heap with the side of his boot. "Ah miss, do you have to tell him?" he asked. "I could right this place in a few minutes and he'd never need to know."

"Of course he has to know! You were drinking and smoking in the barn!"

Fred looked at her steadily for a moment then sighed. "He'll turn me off. Your mother's death on liquor. He'll fire me on the spot."

"Oh no!" gasped Ellen. She had gathered up the half-empty liquor bottle, Fred's pipe and the plate and now stood clutching them as she stared round-eyed at May. "Don't tell, May. Don't have him sent away," she begged.

"He nearly burned down the barn! Killed the cattle! And

those pigs he's so fond of! Do you think they'd have escaped?" She shuddered. "We'd have lost everything, maybe even the house."

"But we didn't," Ellen reminded her. "Fred helped us and we put out the fire. Nothing burned down and no one got hurt."

Still talking, Ellen and Fred went on with the clean-up. May helped them and by the time the barn was tidy again she was weakening. As the two girls prepared for bed Ellen continued to argue with May.

"Why is your mother so down on liquor anyway?" she asked.

"It's because of something that happened in Ontario."

"Before you came here?"

"Before I was even born," answered May. "They just had Sam and Hilda then. Back there, whenever there was a big job to do, like raising a barn, they'd have a bee."

"What's a bee?"

"A work party. All the men would come and help do the work and then there'd be a party afterwards with the women and children. Most of the time there'd be liquor, some men would have too much."

"Not your father!"

"No! Of course not! But one of Mum's cousins did. It seems some of the older men egged on the younger ones and some of them weren't used to it and it made them sort of crazy." She climbed into bed first and took her place against the wall. "Well, one fellow challenged Mum's cousin to an axe-throwing contest and he threw it crooked and it hit a little girl on the head."

"Oh, how awful! Was she killed?"

"Yes. And later the man shot himself."

Ellen shuddered under the blankets. "That's a terrible story. No wonder your Mum hates liquor. But Fred didn't get very drunk and he didn't hurt anyone."

Sometime later, without waking completely, she heard the party-goers return and May calling good night to them. Later still, she was awakened by May screaming in her sleep.

Ellen shook her. "May! Wake up! You're having a nightmare."

May's eyes opened and she sat up in bed, but it was clear she was still seeing whatever had frightened her in her dream. She cried out again.

Mrs. Aitken, wearing a shawl over her nightgown and carrying a candle, came into the room. "What is it, May? What's wrong?"

May threw herself into her mother's arms. "Oh, Mum! Mum! Fred got drunk and burned down the barn!"

"It was only a dream. The barn's still there," said her mother soothingly.

"Fred nearly burned it down," insisted May.

Over her daughter's head, Mrs. Aitkens raised her eyebrows at Ellen.

"No he didn't," Ellen said. "She's having a nightmare."

May pulled out of her mother's arms. She was wide awake now. "Yes he did," she said.

"He didn't nearly burn down the barn," said Ellen scornfully.

"He got drunk!" With the three of them sitting on the bed amid the flickering shadows cast by the candlelight, May told her mother the whole frightening story. Mrs. Aitken's expression became grimmer and grimmer at every word. When May told her how Ellen knew what was wrong with Fred, she said, "Well, if that's the kind of people you lived with in England, you'd better not go back!" Finally she tucked the girls in and went back to her own bed.

In the morning, as Ellen opened the door at the bottom of the stairs, she heard Mrs. Aitken's stern voice. "Pack your bag and get off our land today!"

"Now Charlotte, be reasonable," said her husband in a milder tone. Ellen watched him rub his hand over his bald head. He looked ruefully at Fred, who stood just inside the back door with his cap in his hands.

"Don't you stick up for him Wilfred Aitken! He has to go!"

"I'm not sticking up for him. He was careless. We could have lost everything! But be reasonable. I've no cash on hand to pay him his wages. And where would he go? We must give him a chance to find another situation."

"There's always work to be found at this time of year. He'll soon get another job."

"No doubt. But what about me? How am I to manage the spring work with no help?"

"Don't make difficulties where none exist Wilf!" said his wife. "You take him into town today. Go to the bank and get his wages. Leave word you want help. There's always men and farmers in town looking for one another. You'll both soon get suited. The girls and I will help until you do. I'll not have a man sitting at my table who betrayed my trust!" She turned and rattled the stove lids for a minute. "Come along Ellen," she said. "Sit down to your breakfast. You too May."

When Mr. Aitken was almost ready to leave, Ellen slipped out. She spoke to Fred as he put his old bag into the wagon box.

"I didn't tell," she said.

"I know that," answered Fred.

"It's not fair!" Ellen declared.

Fred shrugged. "Fair? What's fair? Don't you worry. I'll get another job." He put his foot on the hub of the wheel.

"Will I ever see you again?" asked Ellen.

"Maybe," he answered, as he swung into the seat. "I'd like to stay in this district. I like it here. You're the one who's going away."

Mr. Aitken clicked his tongue at the horse and the wagon moved toward the open gate. Ellen followed to close it.

"Give my love to old England when you see it again," said Fred.

At the dip in the road he turned and waved. Ellen swallowed a big lump in her throat.

Chapter 12

As Mrs. Aitken had predicted, her husband was able to bring a new hired man back with him. He was a Swede who spoke very little English. Sven was a hard worker, polite and good-natured, but he wasn't Fred. At first Ellen resented him very much. But as the days passed, she even started to help him learn some English words.

Mr. Aitken overheard her teaching Sven the word *tomah-to* as she pointed out plants in the garden. He laughed. "Look, Ellen, I think you'd better leave the teaching to us Canadians. We don't want him talking like a Limey. That won't do him any good here. The word is *tom-ay-to,* Sven. *Tom-ay-to."* Seeing the hurt look on Ellen's face, he added, "Ah no, Ellen I was only teasing. Don't take it to heart."

But she did take it to heart. Mrs. Aitken criticized her friends. Mr. Aitken criticized her accent. May had betrayed Fred. Even Hilda, who was living at home again, thought about Rudy most of the time. No one seemed to care about her.

On the next Friday afternoon as they walked home from school May noticed a change in the sky. Hilda had gone to stay with Rudy's family for a week, but Ellen, George and Miranda were with her as she began to run.

"Hurry!" she called. "Looks like a hail storm coming. Can you run all the way home Miranda?"

"Yes," said the little girl with a frightened look at the black cloud on the horizon.

"Scoot then! Come on you two."

Before the girls reached home the air had turned cold and five minutes after they burst into the kitchen, hail rattled on the roof and beat against the windows. Ellen found the storm exciting, but she could see that the Aitkens were really worried.

"This could wipe out the crop," explained the farmer. "The hail stones could kill all the new grain shoots."

In a few minutes, the storm passed over.

"That wasn't too bad," said Mrs. Aitken with a sigh of relief.

"Not here," answered her husband, "but somebody got it."

"Bill? Sam?"

"Not Bill. It went north. Sam, maybe. I'll go see."

He was gone almost two hours and they could tell by the way he walked back across the yard that the news was bad.

"Not much damage to us; just a strip along the north fence. But Sam's wiped out. Not a blade standing. We'll have to reseed the whole thing. I'm going over there tomorrow, taking Sven and Prince. Bill will help. We'll stay till we get it in—two days at least. Young George will come here and help you. He can sleep in Sven's room."

Ellen knew how badly upset Mrs. Aitken was on Sunday

morning. Although she usually insisted on everyone keeping the Sabbath very strictly, she never even mentioned the fact that the men would be missing the monthly church service. She just set off walking to the school house with the two girls and George. They arrived just in time to take their places.

As Ellen and George settled on the floor with the other children they heard two men behind them talking.

"Sam Aitken will get reseeded quick enough. He's got his Dad and brother and that Swede Wilf hired."

"What happened to Fred Harper then?"

The first man laughed. "Didn't you hear? They turned him off. For drinking. Yeah, old Fred's gone clean out of the district, way south of Brandon I hear."

"Don't have much luck with their English, do they? They'll never make a farmer out of that orphan they took neither."

"Where's the sense? I ask you! How can you make farmers out of the failures of the cities? Don't make sense. Say, talking about useless English, did you hear about them Winsteads?"

Just then, the minister struck the tuning fork on the desk and everyone stood up to sing 'Holy, Holy, Holy.'

Ellen was so angry she couldn't utter a note. Out of the corner of her eye she could see that George's ears had turned red to the tips. For once, she sympathized with him.

George's anger, however, took in Ellen. He resented the fact that he had not even been given a chance to help with the seeding, but had been sent off to do chores for the women. It seemed to him that Ellen had been accepted and he hadn't been. She wasn't even supposed to be here. If that Hannah hadn't hidden her on the boat when they left Liverpool, she'd be in jail or the workhouse where she belonged.

After the service there was time for visiting with neighbours, catching up on a month's news and finding out what damage the storm had done. Ellen joined Florrie Osborne who was standing with her mother and the Winstead family. The two women were talking about England as though the Winsteads would soon be there.

"Are the Winsteads going home?" Ellen asked Florrie in a whisper.

"Yes, they can't stand it here," Florrie answered in the same low tone. "She hates the weather, the people, the farm, everything! She says she's used to servants, can't stoop to doing things for herself. I wouldn't want to be her servant! They're leaving on the train tonight."

"Tonight!" breathed Ellen, staring at the sour-faced woman jiggling her baby.

"Oh," sighed Mrs. Osborne. "Just think! If England is only a fortnight away, we could be home in Ontario in a week! I almost envy you going home!"

Without realizing how loudly she was speaking, Ellen cried, "I'd love to go home!"

Both the Winsteads threw her startled glances. They looked at one another. Then Mr. Winstead asked, "Do you really want to go to England, Ellen?"

"Yes, I'm going as soon as my uncle sends the money."

"We're going to town now and starting out early tomorrow morning," he answered. "Mrs. Winstead's not looking forward to managing the three youngsters on the voyage. They'll be a handful for her."

He looked at his wife, who answered in a whiny voice, "They'll quite wear me down. I'll be a rag when we arrive home, you know I will Denny."

"Yes dear. So Ellen, would you like to come home with us? We'll pay your fare in exchange for help with the children."

Ellen stared at him with wide eyes, too surprised to speak. Go home to Uncle Bert! Back to Liverpool with the bustle of the city and musical evenings with their friends... leaving the farm, the open spaces, school, Sky. She couldn't leave her kitten! Just then loud laughter came from a group of men near the school fence. They were probably laughing about the English again.

"Yes, I'll go with you," she said aloud.

"Splendid!" said Mr. Winstead.

"I'm glad," echoed his wife. "You can come with us now and stay in the boarding house. The train leaves at two o'clock in the morning. You may have Jenny's clothes. She's the servant we brought with us. The one who left after three months." Her face hardened at the memory. "Naturally, since she hadn't fulfilled her contract, I kept the clothes. She was just about your size so they'll fit." Turning to her husband, she exclaimed, "Oh Denny, to have a Nanny for the children! Go and speak to Mrs. Aitken immediately."

But Mrs. Aitken had been offered a ride home and left the others to walk. May looked astonished as Ellen and Mr. Winstead told of their plan.

"Go home to your uncle? Now?" she exclaimed. "But Ellen, he won't be expecting you. How will he know where to meet you?"

"That's all right young lady," said Mr. Winstead. "We're sailing on the *Caroline* and she docks in Liverpool. I won't leave Ellen until I see her reunited with her uncle, you can assure your parents of that."

May frowned. "I wish they were here! Or Hilda! They'd know what was best. Ellen, I really think that you should wait for your uncle to send the money for your fare."

"But May!" wailed Ellen, "It may take months longer! I can be with him in a fortnight!"

"That's what she thinks," muttered Michael, who was standing nearby.

Only George heard him. "What?" he asked.

"They ain't going home to England right away," the younger boy answered in a whisper. "I heard her talking to Mum. They're going to stay two months or so visiting in Toronto with his cousins. They want a servant so's to leave the kids while they gallivants around with their swell friends. She won't be seeing no uncle in two weeks."

Serves her right, thought George. He knew he should tell May what he had just heard. But if he did, she would not let Ellen leave with the Winsteads and Ellen really wanted to go home to England. What did it matter that she wouldn't be going quite as soon as she expected?

May sighed. "Well, I can't stop you. We'll miss you—all of us." Ellen smiled a bit tearfully. "Mind you write as soon as you get there," added May more briskly. "Mum'll be worried about you."

"I will! Thank you for everything—all of you. And May, take care of Sky please."

May, looking both hurt and angry, just nodded.

George hardly spoke to May on the long walk home. His thoughts swung from gloating over Ellen's disappointment when she found she would be three months on the way to wondering whether he should tell what he knew. It's too late, he thought. With Mr. Aitken and the horse gone there's no way to get her back.

Mr. Aitken and Sven returned with Prince just as it got dark.

"No need for you to go back right away George," the farmer said. "Stay the night." He hung his hat behind the door. "We sure appreciate you coming to help with the chores. It meant we could get that job done in jig time."

As they all sat down for a bed-time cup of tea, May told again about Ellen and the Winsteads.

"I just can't believe it! Ellen gone!" her father said. "It'll sure seem strange without her. I never thought she'd just up and leave us like that. I thought she liked us."

"Wilf, don't blame May," said his wife. "It does seem such a good chance for the child—her fare paid and decent people to travel with." She began to gather up the dishes, rattling them more than necessary.

"Oh, I'm not blaming anyone Charlotte. I just wish that it wasn't the Winsteads she was going with."

"I just wish she'd waited," said May. "It might not have been so long till her uncle sent for her."

George groaned. The money might come and Ellen would be stuck in Toronto with them Winsteads and he'd be blamed. He blurted out what Michael had told him.

"Well, now," said Mr. Aitken, rubbing his head with both hands.

"We can't let her go!" exclaimed May.

Mrs. Aitken dropped her dishcloth and plopped down again at the table. "You'll have to go into town, Wilf, and be sure that Ellen understands they're not going right home."

"It's about four hours before the train leaves," said May. "It only takes a bit over two hours to get to town, say two and a half in the dark. May I go with you?"

"No. I'd like your mother to come in case the Winsteads try to keep her. Will you Charlotte?" His wife nodded. "Good!" The worried frown left his forehead and his blue eyes brightened. "Ellen's much better off here until her uncle sends for her. He'll think we're poor guardians of the girl, allowing her to go off like that."

In twenty minutes George and May waved goodbye as Prince drew the buggy toward the farm gate. Sven was standing there ready to close it after them.

"We'll take care of things here," May called. "You just bring Ellen back."

"If she wants to come," her mother answered.

She was perched on the seat, looking at the youngsters barely visible in the lantern light. She didn't notice that her husband was driving too close to the gate post. When the hub of the wheel caught on the post, a worn pin gave way and the wheel fell off. The buggy lurched to the right and she was flung out on to the hard ground.

Sven grabbed the bridle rein of the frightened horse and stopped him from rocking the buggy. Mr. Aitken slid down the sloping seat and ran to his wife. May had lifted her mother into sitting position. By the light of George's lantern they saw that Charlotte's hat was askew and the right side of her face badly scraped by the ridged clay.

"Are you hurt?" her husband asked.

"Yes I think so," she answered quietly. She ran her left

hand slowly down her right arm and winced with pain when she reached the wrist. "I don't think it's broken," she said. "A bad sprain perhaps and my ankle's twisted. I'm afraid I can't go to town."

"No, no of course not. Let's get you into the house."

She allowed him to help her up, but took May's arm instead of his. "Can you fix the buggy?" she asked.

"It would take too long," he answered.

"Then you must go in the wagon. Take May with you."

"Mister!" called Sven from the darkness beyond the circle of lantern light. "Nobody go. Horse lame."

"What?" He hurried to examine Prince. "You're right," he said.

For a moment they all stood in stunned silence. May was the first to speak. "It's all your fault George!" she said with a sob.

"Crying won't help!" said her mother sternly. "Help me inside.

"Bill will have to go," said Mr. Aitken. "George, you run over to his place and tell him what's happened. He can go to town on Ebony." As the boy started off he called, "Take John A. with you."

"And be careful!" called Mrs. Aitken, in a pain-filled voice. "It won't help Ellen if you break a leg in a gopher hole."

John A. was excited at the novelty of a night romp. At first, George tried to keep up with his speed, but quickly realized the truth of Mrs. Aitken's remark when he nearly tripped. It was long past Bill's bedtime and George and John A. had a hard time waking him and making him understand. When he did, he dressed quickly and routed out old Ebony.

"Climb on George," he said. "I'll take you home."

"There isn't time," exclaimed George. "Just hurry to town!"

"If you're talking to Ebony my boy you might as well save your breath. He never hurries anywhere."

"But he will get there before the train comes in won't he?"

"He will," answered Bill.

Ebony did make good time for the first few miles. Then he began to limp. Bill slid from his back and carefully examined all four limbs.

"There's nothing wrong with you," he said, climbing back on. "Just keep going! It must be past midnight already."

With less than an hour to train time and miles still to go, he kicked Ebony hard on both flanks. "Move! No more play acting! We'll miss Ellen and she'll be stuck with the Winsteads."

Molly, the maid at the boarding house, had used almost the same words at supper earlier in the evening. She flounced into the kitchen where Ellen was eating with the cook, since Mrs. Winstead did not sit down to meals with servants.

Brandishing the teapot, she said, "The tea's too weak for her ladyship, Mrs. Bead."

"Too weak, is it?" answered Mrs. Bead, heaving herself out of her chair. "This afternoon it was too strong! There's no pleasing some people." She threw a handful of tea leaves into the pot. "Ach, well, it's only today we have to put up with her. By two o'clock tomorrow morning they'll be gone."

Molly looked at Ellen. "Yes. And am I glad that she's found a nursemaid and it ain't me will have to get them brats up and dressed for the train. How ever will you stand being stuck with them?"

"Oh well," answered Ellen, "I'm only staying with them till we get to Liverpool. Three weeks isn't so long."

The cook and maid exchanged glances. Mrs. Bead shook her head firmly and Molly went back to the dining room with the teapot and a plate of bread. Ellen knew that the two women thought she was foolish to be leaving the Aitkens for the Winsteads.

At one o'clock in the morning, when Mr. Winstead tapped on the door of the attic room to waken her, she tiptoed out of the room without disturbing Molly. Downstairs, Ellen found the children fretful and frightened of the dark. It took all her attention to get them dressed and ready. Mrs. Winstead was almost as fretful as the children. She scolded Ellen because she was slow. She scolded the horseman because the road was bumpy. She scolded the station master because their baggage had been left out on the platform.

"What's the harm?" he asked. "It's a perfectly clear night. See the stars?"

She sniffed and turned away. There was only one other person on the platform, the Anglican priest who had come to meet his son. He hurried forward and escorted Mrs. Winstead and the baby to the bench under the lantern. Ellen lifted the other two children up beside their mother and stood beside them.

"So you're leaving us," he said. "Well, do have a happy time in the east before you sail. I almost envy you. Three months in Toronto! And with friends to show you around. Ah, excuse me. There's the whistle. My horse always takes fright at the train."

He hurried off and Ellen turned wide eyes to Mr. Winstead.

"Three months in Toronto?" she asked. "You said you were going home."

"So we are," he answered. "After we've spent some time with friends in the east."

"Three months! I can't go! Uncle Bert won't know where I am. He'll send the money and I won't be here."

"Hold Jules, Ellen," said Mrs. Winstead sharply. "He might fall on to the track."

The huge locomotive thundered past and drew the passenger coach to a screeching halt opposite them.

"I can't go with you!" repeated Ellen desperately.

Mr. Winstead shepherded them toward the conductor at the foot of the coach steps.

"You'll have to come," he answered. "Where else would you go? The Aitkens won't take you back after you ran out on them."

Suddenly, Ellen felt an arm across her shoulders. "They certainly will take her back," said Bill. "They're all waiting right now for me to bring her home."

"See here Aitken," said Mr. Winstead. "We hired Ellen as a nursemaid. She agreed to come to England with us."

"Only because she thought she'd be with her uncle soon. That was a sneaky trick you played—not telling her you were going to be three months on the way."

The train whistle sounded, drowning out Mr. Winstead's reply.

"All aboard!" called the conductor.

The Englishman looked from the conductor to Ellen. Then he swung his children up the steps and urged his wife after them. As the train began to move, Ellen and Bill heard her whining, "But what am I going to do with the children Denny?"

Bill grinned down at Ellen. "The last time I picked you up at the station you had to ride in a wagon. That was bad enough. This time I've only got old Ebony. Do you want to stay in town and wait for Dad to come with the buggy?"

"Let's go home," said Ellen.

Chapter 13

The warm weather continued and by the middle of June the wild grass and clover were ready to be harvested for hay. One Saturday morning Mr. Aitken walked over to Bill's place to make plans for beginning the haying on Monday morning. On his return, instead of using the road he plodded along the edge of the pasture checking the fence for broken wire or rotted posts. Just as he entered the copse of poplar trees a meadow lark poured out its lilting song. It was perched on a fence post beside a wild rose bush. Someone else had stopped to listen. A man walking on the road had set down his burdens and stood with his head tilted. He was too far away to see clearly but the farmer knew he was a stranger.

The bird flew off and the man stooped and wearily picked up his bundles. He couldn't seem to decide whether to walk in the deep wheel rut or on the grassy ridge in the centre of the road, but kept changing from one to the other. He walked like a man whose feet were sore.

A city man, thought Mr. Aitken, smiling at the bowler hat and gloves the man wore. Probably looking for work. Won't be much use I suppose. Maybe he can drive the rick. The man switched his two pieces of baggage from one hand to the other. One was a long duffel bag and the other looked like a violin case. The farmer slipped further behind a tree and squinted as he studied the stranger. Could it be? It must be! He began to stride through the wood. If he cut across the upper field, he'd be at the house a good ten minutes before the stranger.

As he strode into the kitchen, Ellen was at the stove mashing potatoes. "Ellen," he said, "I saw your cat on the road, way off near the south fence post. You'd better go and fetch her."

His wife straightened up from the oven with the roast pan in her hands and turned to him in astonishment. "Fetch the cat? Nonsense, Wilf! We're about to dish up. The cat will come home by itself."

Her husband gave her a look that plainly said to let Ellen go.

"Dad," began May, "Sky is..."

The fierce frown she received left her with her mouth open.

"Go on, Ellen," said Mr. Aitken.

Ellen ran out the door, across the yard and through the gate on to the road. As she came to the top of the slight rise, she gazed anxiously ahead. She saw no cat, but she did see a man walking towards her.

Her eyes opened wide, she stumbled for a step or two and then flew along the road. The man dropped his baggage and opened his arms. She collapsed into them.

"Uncle Bert! What are you doing here? How did you get here?" Ellen was laughing and crying at once.

"Came to see you. By ship, train, wagon to the crossroads back there and shank's mare this far," answered her uncle with a grin, slapping his leg.

"But why? Why?" she exclaimed. "I thought you were going to send me the money to go home." Her hands flew up to cover her mouth and she stared over them with wide eyes. Her legs trembled. "I nearly went back with the Winsteads! I nearly missed you!"

"Look Nellie," said Bert, "do you think we could sit down somewhere? My feet are killing me!"

"Oh I'm sorry! Yes." She picked up the violin case. "We'll go to the house. The Aitkens will be surprised to see you."

Holding his bag in one hand and his niece's hand in the other, Herbert Winter limped up to the farm house where Ellen had spent the long months she'd been separated from him. He was soon made comfortable with his tight shoes replaced by felt slippers and his hunger satisfied by a huge farm dinner. Only then did he get around to answering Ellen's question.

Mr. Aitken repeated it. "Why did you come out? We thought you'd be sending for Ellen to go home."

"It was the picture," said the Englishman. "When I saw that picture Ellen sent me, I could hardly believe it. Well, I thought, that place evidently suits my Nellie. Those folks must be awfully good to her. So I said to myself, why not go out there and see how it would be for me? I hadn't got very far saving money. I thought maybe I had half of what I would need. Fortunately, one of the chaps I know told me that the steamer *Orpheus* needed a replacement violin in the string quartet that played in the posh dining salon. As soon as he said they landed in Quebec, I rushed down and saw the purser. I got the job because I was willing to leave the next day."

"Just like me," interrupted Ellen. "You just set off."

"Only I went willingly," laughed her uncle. "Yes, I had to do some scrambling, but I made it. Had a free bed and all my meals so it didn't cost me a shilling to cross the ocean. Then in Quebec I sold my flute to pay for lodgings while I found out how to travel further west. Then I plunked down most of my money for train fare and here I am."

Mrs. Aitken signalled to May to start clearing the table. "And what did you intend to do in Canada Mr. Winter?" she asked.

"Well Ma'am, the first thing, naturally, was to find Ellen and I've done that. Next will be to find a place to live and a job I suppose."

"You'll stay with us for a while of course," Mr. Aitken said. "If you want a job, I can put you to work helping with the haying. My son Bill and I are starting Monday morning."

Herbert smiled at him. "I've never done any haying, but I'm sure willing to try. Thanks."

Because Sunday was a day of rest, Bert had time to recover from his long walk. That evening, Sam and his family, Bill, the Ransome boys and Rudy all dropped in to meet Ellen's uncle from England. She gloated as she introduced him to George.

"Uncle Bert, this is George Matthews. He's one of the *orphans* I came out to Canada with." A little later, she drew

George into a corner. "See George Matthews, I do so have an uncle! So there!" She stuck out her tongue at him.

"Yeah!" retorted George, "but you're not going back to England!"

"I don't want to," declared Ellen. "Not now that my uncle is here."

She nearly burst with pride when he played the violin and they all clapped loudly.

The next day Bert found that haying was very hard work. And to Ellen's shame, after three days of being kind till he got used to it, Bill declared the Bert Winter was the worst farm hand he'd ever seen. The horses refused to obey him, so he couldn't be given the soft job of driving the rick. The pitchfork made his hands raw with blisters. Every evening Ellen bathed them with warm water and baking soda and wrapped them in soft cloths. In the field he kept stopping to wipe the sweat from his face or stretch the crick in his back. This disrupted the rhythm and timing of the other men who were loading the wagon with sweet smelling hay. When they put him on top of the wagon to spread the bundles they tossed up, he had a hard time keeping up.

Even though Bill lost his temper once or twice, Bert remained cheerful through it all. By the time Sunday rolled around again, the hay was all safely in and the Englishman had definitely made up his mind not to be a farmer.

It was Ellen's idea anyway. "Sven wants to leave soon Uncle Bert," she had said. "You could take his job, then we could both live here with the Aitkens through the winter and next spring you could get a homestead like Bill."

After dinner on the next Sunday, everyone scattered.

May walked over to Sam's to play with Teddy. Hilda went for a drive with Rudy. Mr. Aitken settled in his chair in the kitchen for a nap while Sven snoozed in his room. Mrs. Aitken wrote letters in the parlour and Ellen and her uncle sat in the shade of the lilac tree in the yard. It was the first chance they had found for a long talk. Ellen expertly built a smudge to keep off the mosquitoes. They talked eagerly for an hour about all that had happened to them in the months since Ellen had sailed away from the Liverpool dock. Twice they had to move as the shade shifted and three times Ellen added grass to the smudge.

She lay back on the lawn and sighed happily.

Herbert had been propped on one elbow beside her. He now sat up straight and looked at her sideways with a serious expression. "The thing is Nell, what next? I can't stay here."

"Not even for the summer?" she asked wistfully.

He made a face. "What would I do? I'm no good to Mr. Aitken. Besides, I hate farming!" He gave a little laugh. "You know I've never liked hard work."

Ellen smiled back fondly. "But you work hard at your music."

"That's different. I love that."

His niece sighed. "So where will we go? Back to England?"

"No. I want to try life in Canada first. I thought I'd go to Winnipeg and look for a job there. There's a train from town early tomorrow morning they tell me. Bill has offered to drive me in."

Ellen sat up. "That doesn't give me much time to get ready! Almost like leaving England!" She looked around at the house, the farm buildings, the fields. "I'll be sorry to leave all this, but as long as we're together, that's what matters."

Herbert hugged his knees and stared down at his boot tops. "The thing is Nellie, I want you to stay here."

She shivered as though a cold wind had passed over her. "Stay here? You mean till you get settled. How long do you think that will be?"

He turned an unhappy face toward her, "Nellie, I mean live here—not come with me at all."

Her body felt leaden. A mosquito landed on her arm and although she was aware of the sting, she couldn't even raise her hand to swat it.

Her uncle hurried on. "I've nothing to offer you, Ellen. No place to live, no money to live on. I'll make out but it's no life for a girl. Here, you've got a good home." His voice took on a coaxing tone. "You like it here; you told me so. And the Aitkens want you."

Ellen sprang up and stared at him with blazing eyes. "And you don't want me!" she shouted. "It's just like Miss Fawcett said. You were glad to get rid of me." Her voice broke on a sob.

"Now Nellie, didn't I come all the way to Canada to see you?"

But the girl was not listening. She whirled around and ran from the yard and down the road. Blinded by tears, she stumbled into her secret place in the poplar bluff and crept in among the trees. Under their shelter she lay on the ground and cried. She really was an orphan!

From the parlour, Mrs. Aitken had heard Ellen's raised voice. She came out and stood beside the young man. "Did you tell her?" she asked.

He nodded. "She took it awfully bad. I'd better go after her."

"No, don't do that. Not just now. Let her have her cry out. There's a place she sits to be alone, among the trees down the road. Talk to her again when she's got used to the idea. Ellen's a sensible girl. She'll see what's best. Come inside now and I'll make a cup of tea. Isn't that supposed to be the cure-all in England?"

Hilda had been worried about how Ellen would take the news. She persuaded Rudy to bring her back early. She found Herbert in the yard, half-hidden by the lilac bush.

"Do you think I should go to her?" she asked.

"I wish you would," he answered gratefully.

By the time Hilda peered into the tiny clearing, Ellen had stopped crying. She sat propped up against a tree trunk staring straight ahead.

"May I come in?" asked Hilda in her softest voice.

Ellen looked up and nodded. Hilda almost cried out at the pain in the child's eyes. She sat down and took her hand.

After a moment Ellen said, "Uncle Bert wants to go away and leave me."

"I know."

Ellen snatched her hand away.

"Did you all know?" cried Ellen. "All except me?"

"Your uncle had to talk it over with Mum and Dad, Ellen. You know Mum, she wanted to be sure he could take care of you. Your uncle of course needed to know whether they really wanted you to live with them."

"But he doesn't want me!" Ellen had no tears left. "He doesn't love me," she said bleakly.

Hilda put her arm around the child's shoulders. "Of course he does Ellen. Anyone looking at you two can see that he loves you very much."

"Then why won't he take me with him?"

Hilda did not answer for a few minutes. When she spoke it was very earnestly. "You see Ellen, when you love someone, you want what's best for that person. Your uncle came all this way to find you because he loves you and wants to be with you. Then he discovered that you would be better off on the farm than you would be in the city with him. And so he gave up his dream of the two of you living together again."

Ellen pushed away from the older girl and scratched on the ground with a stick. "Ever since I left Liverpool that day, I've wanted to get back to him. And now it's happened and he doesn't want me."

"He does want you Ellen. Very much. I know that it was very hard for him to decide to leave you again. He's doing it because he loves you."

When Ellen turned to look at her, Hilda met her eyes steadily. She gave a little smile, but Ellen did not respond.

"Dear Ellen," said Hilda, "we love you too. And we want you. When May leaves in the fall to go to high school Mum and Dad will be awfully lonely without a daughter. You see, by that time, Rudy and I will be married."

Ellen's eyes brightened at that. "Really?" she asked.

"Yes, really. And good gracious, how could we get married without you singing at the wedding? Rudy would think it wasn't legal!"

Ellen blinked away tears and gave a little hiccup. She allowed Hilda to stroke her hair.

"Let's go home, Ellen. Your uncle is awfully worried."

They walked hand in hand back to where Herbert was waiting.

"Forgive me for upsetting you, Nellie," he said with a lop-sided grin. "I was only trying to do what's right for you. You didn't let me finish all I meant to say. I love you very much and of course, if you want to, you can come with me."

"Let's not decide anything this minute," said Hilda briskly. "Supper must be ready. Since this is your last night Mr. Winter, let's have some music afterwards."

"Can't play the violin with these hands," he answered ruefully, "but there's nothing wrong with my voice."

After supper they did sing a few hymns, but nobody's heart was in it. Ellen kept looking at the others wondering what they were thinking. Earlier, while they did the dishes, May had said, "I want you to stay, Ellen. I really do."

Every time she looked at Mr. Aitken he winked at her, caught his lower lip in his teeth and shrugged one shoulder. Finally at eight o'clock, Mrs. Aitken rolled up her knitting, placed it on the table and rested her hands on it.

"Ellen," she said, "you must make up your mind now whether you're going with your uncle. If you are, we'll have to get your things packed." She paused and no one moved or spoke. They hardly seemed to breathe. "You're welcome to stay. All of us want you to. But it's up to you. Your uncle is family and that's important, we know."

Mr. Aitken rubbed his head. "I've come to think of you as part of this family, Ellen," he said.

Hilda and May both nodded.

Ellen looked at the circle of caring faces. She remembered

Hilda's words. *When you love someone, you do what's best for them.* Right now, she would only be a burden to her uncle.

"I'll stay," she said.